SHOTGUN

A Novella by Don Neal

First Edition Design Publishing
Sarasota, Florida USA

Shotgun
Copyright ©2020 Don Neal

ISBN 978-1506-909-72-1 PBK
ISBN 978-1506-909-73-8 EBK

LCCN 2020918810

December 2020

Published and Distributed by
First Edition Design Publishing, Inc.
P.O. Box 17646, Sarasota, FL 34276-3217
www.firsteditiondesignpublishing.com

To Deborah and Cheryl, my most faithful fans.

SEWARD, ALASKA; JUNE, 1975

ZOOP, ZOOP, ZOOP

Peter Paul Peterson was a very impressive guy. Well over six feet from toe to top, well-muscled in between, black hair clipped short in the latest movie "bad guy" style; he was 230 pounds of pure meanness. At present, most of his 230 pounds were concentrated on the hacksaw which he was pumping against the shotgun barrels braced under his left knee. The blade, which had been singing a rhythmic "zoop, zoop, zoop" as it chewed its way through the tough steel of the 12-gauge barrels, began changing pitch toward an irritating "scree, scree, scree" as its teeth wore away. Pete, who was a perfect example of the military BFFI principle, immediately compensated by adding more of his 230 pounds to the pressure on the blade.

BFFI was a term originated by soldiers, normally used in conjunction with references to the Marine Corps, which stood for "Brute Force and Fucking Ignorance".

"Tink!", "Gahhh!", "Wham!", "Crash!", "Thunk!"

"Tink!" was the snapping of the over-stressed hacksaw blade, which had been too loosely attached in the first place.

"Gahhh!" was the roar emitted by Pete after his knuckles smashed against the barrels under 230 pounds of weight.

"Wham!" was the hacksaw slamming into the far wall as Pete flung it across the room.

"Crash!" was the hanging picture of Alaska's ex-governor, Bill Egan, as it fell to the floor and shattered.

"Thunk!" was the sound of the front door slamming as Sam Duncan hurriedly left the cabin before Pete could see him grinning.

Sam, who was sandy-haired, of average height and on the chubby side, was no fighter. And he was well aware that anyone caught laughing at Pete

Peterson had best be a helluva fighter or a very fast runner. Being neither, Sam survived by maintaining a poker face and strict neutrality.

Sam had no liking for, and a great deal of fear of Pete. He stayed in the cabin with Pete for the same reason that a magpie hangs around a wolf pack—easy meals for which someone else has done the work and planning. Although he had never directly thought about the matter, his philosophy might have been, "Easier to be a gofer for an asshole than to work one's own way through life."

The third member of the trio was already sitting on the front deck of the cabin. He had heard enough of the bedlam inside to know that innocent ignorance was probably the safest demeanor for the moment.

Eddy Hoyt was a small person when compared with Pete Peterson or Sam Duncan, but he had made use of that disparity by learning to be a small target. Eddy was one of those diminutive people who could remain unnoticed in a room full of nuns. He was the face in a crowd that no one could quite remember, even though they might have had a lengthy conversation with him moments before. Wiry, in his early thirties with thinning dark hair, Eddy was the introvert of the trio.

Eddy, Sam, and Pete formed the household of the shacky cabin in which they lived; one that they had found temporarily unoccupied and had appropriated for their own use.

When the cabin door flew open a few seconds later, Pete's angry gaze slid completely over Eddy, as usual, and fastened on Sam.

"Sam, run into Seward and pick up a couple of hacksaw blades."

"Hell, Pete, I only got five bucks."

"That oughtta be enough. Git!"

"OK. Gimme the keys to the truck."

"Sam, the last thing we need is for you to get picked up tooling around town in a hot truck. Hike!"

"Well, why'd we boost it if we can't drive it?"

Pete seemed to swell like a puff adder.

"Two reasons. First, we wanna keep it outta sight until the day of the job. Second, 'cause if you don't start walking right now, I'm gonna reach up your ass, grab you by the tongue, and jerk you inside out!"

Sam hastily started up the dirt lane.

"Right. I'm on it, Pete— no problem."

BLADES OR BEER

Sam Duncan was what past generations would have called a "ne'er do well". In his case, however, it wasn't because he wasn't able to do well—more that he didn't take the trouble to try. The youngest of three brothers, Sam had gotten used to being coddled as a child and watched over protectively by his big brothers during his boyhood. His middle-class parents good-naturedly ignored those of his misdemeanors which came to their attention, most having been covered up by his brothers.

Sam grew up to be an amiable chap, pleasant enough to have around that his laziness was tolerated and his lack of ambition forgiven. As a man, he became a likable and very skillful free-loader, attaching himself to whichever person or group provided him with the most fringe benefits for the least output of energy. At present, Pete did the thinking and planning for the trio, while Sam performed simple assigned tasks in turn for bread, beer, and any other fruit that fell from the Pete tree.

Sam slogged the mile of dirt road to the highway and positioned himself for hitch-hiking into Seward, a short three miles down the road. Whenever he heard a vehicle coming, he began walking toward town with a practiced weary gate designed to soften the most calloused heart. If passed up, he stopped walking and contemplated the beauties of the day.

Sam had long ago studied the dynamics of hitch-hiking, and had decided that if one walked toward his destination and were eventually picked up, any walking that had been done was wasted effort. Never one to waste effort, Sam walked only as much as needed to convince drivers that he was a poor footsore working stiff who really deserved a lift.

This particular day did have its beauties to contemplate. The late June sun had, for once, no clouds shielding it. Seward, often gray and damp in early summer, was a thoroughly delightful town when the weather allowed. About the only discordant feature was the powerful aroma emitted by a local fish processing plant. Even this became a mere background scent after one had been in town for an hour or two and had his nostrils thoroughly cauterized by constant exposure.

Sam had caught a ride almost immediately, having wasted only a tiny bit of effort in walking. In town, he alighted from an old Dodge pickup, thanked the driver humbly, and sought out the hardware store. Fate had surely smiled on Sam this day; the hardware store stood two doors down from a notions store and across the street from a bar.

On the way into town, he had carefully considered the relative benefits of hacksaw blades, surely to be shortly broken, and a cold beer. The beer would certainly refresh him for the long walk back to the cabin, but the blades would save him from a painful encounter with Pete. The best outcome, of course was to have both, and the only way to have both was not to pay for one. Since it was very unlikely that he could steal a beer from an alert bartender, it followed that he must steal the hacksaw blades.

Five minutes later he emerged from the hardware store bathed in the smug satisfaction of a job well done. He removed his arm from the sling he had fashioned from a large bandana pilfered from the notions store, removed the packet of blades from up his sleeve, and secured both in the pockets of his jacket. The beer tasted great.

ANCHORAGE, ALASKA; JUNE 1975

TAKE A HIKE!

I was starting to get antsy while waiting for Liz's next visit to Anchorage. After she was transferred to the FBI office in Norfolk, my life seemed to have faded from technicolor to sepia-tone. One memorable night, after a long year's absence, she had returned on a duty assignment. Our reunion, and its climactic ending, had convinced us both that we belonged together, both in spirit and in body.

Liz, FBI Agent Elise Nichole, to use her full nomenclature, then worked out a plan by which she would take a week of leave every three months and visit me in Alaska. If her duties as an FBI agent interfered, I might overcome my aversion to civilization and its crowds and visit her in Virginia.

Being a retired soldier, "Major" Benjamin T. Hunnicutt, no less, I was more or less free to schedule my life as I wished. Living in Alaska in the 1970s was expensive—everything one bought had "freight added" on its price tag. But being a bachelor, owning my modest home via a few lucky breaks, and ever ready to take seasonal advantage of the fish and game available, I made out rather well.

I had just returned from my annual visit to the near-ghost town of Chitina to dip-net Copper River red salmon. Twenty fat fish rested (in peace, I hoped) in the chest freezer in the garage. Since I only ate fish every week or so, the Chitina fishery took care of most of my finned needs for the year. Sport-caught fish filled in the rest, and in late summer and fall caribou would contribute to my meat supply. Careless spruce grouse feeding near the back roads often plugged the gaps in my larder.

With no subsistence chores awaiting and Liz's visit still a few weeks away, I decided to take a week in the mountains away from Anchorage and its bustling, pipeline-invigorated economy. Blessed though the oil boom might be to the civilizing of the state, many of us saw it as the beginning of the end of Frontier Alaska as we knew it. I took advantage of any and every excuse to flee to the back country.

I had spent a lot of time in Cooper Landing during the 1950s, recruiting and organizing the Stay-Behind Agents that were trained and equipped to help in the retaking of the Territory if Russia decided to move in while our armed forces were busy elsewhere. Russia never did, of course, but the friends I had made at that time were still my friends, and I felt a home-like attachment to the entire Kenai Peninsula. When I had the urge to take to the mountains, I generally gravitated south toward Cooper Landing, using it as a starting place.

Although I'd fished the Russian River at Cooper Landing, I had never explored the trail leading upstream along the Russian Lakes and beyond. In theory, it should meet the beginnings of the Resurrection River and its corresponding trail which began in the mountains south of Cooper Landing. That trail traced the river southward to where it dumped into Resurrection Bay near Seward—at least, that's what the maps hinted.

Seward hosts a footrace every Fourth of July—a race which involves climbing nearly straight up Mount Marathon, right next door to downtown Seward. About 70 or 80 fanatics race from the town's center to a peak on the mountain and back down. The distance is over three miles, round trip; the altitude gain, about 3000 feet, of which nearly 2700 are gained in one mile. In places, it's necessary to climb using all-fours, and during the descent it's not unusual for runners to slide, bounce, or roll 30 or 40 feet at a stretch. Most are bleeding somewhere when they cross the finish line.

Never having seen folks attempt such feats of daring and folly unless they were being shot at, I thought the Seward race should be interesting to watch—from level ground.

I made arrangements with Gary Brandt, a friend in Seward—I would drive my truck down to leave with him the week before the race. Gary would then ferry me up to Cooper Landing where I'd overnight in the loft of Bill Fuller's Gunsmithing Shop. I'd start my trek up the Russian River trail the next morning, hoping to make it over to the Resurrection Trail and down to Seward in time to watch the race on Friday. I figured on three days if things went right, but allowed for five since the southern trail was little used and vaguely mapped.

THE JOB

Sam arrived back at the cabin during late afternoon. His beer had led to a friendly conversation with a long-line fisherman who, having come into port with a full fish hold, was feeling generous and companionable. This had led to a few more beers, all free, so Sam had walked the entire way back hoping to dissipate the fumes and avoid Pete's anger.

As Sam entered the cabin door, Pete wordlessly snatched the blades from his fingers and attacked the unfortunate shotgun with renewed vigor. After several slips and another mangled finger, he cursed everyone present and the horses they rode in on, putting aside the 12-gauge circumcision project for the time being.

"Pete, tell us about that job you lined up for us," said Sam, slightly emboldened by the remnants of his beer high. "If we gotta hang around this shack for weeks watching you hack on that damn shotgun, we oughta know why."

"It's a big money job," said Pete, "and that's all you gotta know for now. I been thinking about it for months, and the perfect time's coming up."

"If it needs a sawed-off shotgun," said Eddy, "it sounds hairy. I don't wanna get mixed up in any damn Dodge City shoot-out."

"Me neither," said Sam. "I don't minding boosting stuff off the docks, or a little breaking-in if the pay's good, but armed robbery can get outta hand fast. Getting caught gets you a long spell in the brig. And that sawed-off," he nodded at the mutilated weapon lying on the table, "gets the Feds in the picture."

Pete could hear their enthusiasm beginning to wane, and he knew he needed both of them to carry out the project he had in mind. Against his better judgement, if any part of his judgement could be could be called better, he sighed and sat down on the iron bed in the corner.

"Okay, if you must know. We got one bank in Seward—that branch of the First National that's down on 4th Street where it crosses Adams. It's a regular small-town bank, no real security and maybe one guard on special occasions."

"A bank job!" interrupted Sam. "Hell, Pete, that'll get the Feds down on us. Last thing we need is the IRS and FBI chasing us around Alaska."

"I don't think we gotta worry about the IRS unless you plan to pay taxes on the money," said Pete. "and by the time the Feebies get here, we'll be somewhere else rolling in cash."

"No way!" said Sam, casting his fear of Pete to the winds. "I'm not getting into the armed robbery business and tangling with the Feds just for a few thousand bucks."

"Well, you're right about that," said Pete. "I wouldn't either. But this isn't for a few thousand bucks."

He sat back and counted his selling points off on his fingers.

"First, we got the commercial fishing season going on, and the bank loads up on money for paying off the fishermen when they come in to cash their fish tickets.

"Second, we got the fish processors running wide open, and the bank has to have cash on hand to cover their payrolls.

"Third, we got that crazy Mount Marathon Race on the Fourth when the town fills up with eye-ballers and tourists. The bank sends out for more money to cover that."

There was silence as his listeners absorbed the implications of the three fingers Pete was still holding in the air.

"Jeez, Pete—how much do you think they'll have in the vault?" asked Eddy, who been quiet until now.

"According to a guy I talked to yesterday, 250 grand came in by train last week. Add that to whatever's in the vault; it's sure worth taking a swing at. You wanna try dividing a half mil by three and see if you think it's worth a little risk?"

A shorter silence.

"I'm in," said Sam.

"How we gonna do it?" asked Eddy.

THE RUSSIAN TRAIL

I got a later start on the trail than I had intended. After Gary dropped me off at Cooper Landing and I had stowed my gear in the shop, Bill and I had lounged around talking about important matters such as river boats, all-terrain vehicles, and the easiest way to butcher a moose. We had about exhausted these subjects when Mike Lineman, a local member of the shooting clan, came in, rifle in hand, asking Bill's permission to fire a few shots to test some new handloads in his old Sharps.

The discussion of Mike's antique rifle, the loads he was going to test, and a re-hash of the original three subjects occupied the next hour; the test firing itself, with the usual unsolicited advice from us bystanders, filled the time until supper was announced by Betty Fuller. Although my presence was unplanned (I had figured to eat at Gwin's Lodge, just up the road), to refuse her offer would have been an insult—plus, she was a helluva cook. Mike cleaned his rifle in the shop and went home, promising to return later for more conversation.

When he returned later and heard about my planned hike, he immediately suggested I start from the Cooper Lake trail, which was above the Upper Russian Lakes Trail and saved about 10 miles of walking up from the Russian River.

The Russian River was full of fish, jammed with fishermen, and sprinkled with hungry and impatient bears. Walking south from there would involve mingling with all three nuisances—meeting the trail higher up would certainly save miles, muscle, and probably some degree of annoyance.

Mike picked me up at the shop late in the morning and hauled me and my gear back to Snug Harbor Road and up toward Cooper Lake. It was a beautiful morning, the east flank of Cooper Mountain overlooked the dirt road on which we drove, which in turn overlooked the sparkling turquoise waters of Kenai Lake. As we approached the uphill curve toward Cooper Lake, I recognized the spot off to the left where, back in the 1950s, one of my Stay-Behind Agents had built his survival cache in a thick spruce forest. Ab Gilliland, a professional bush pilot, had been one of the first agents I had recruited; killed in a plane crash some years later, he still had kinfolk in the area.

My mind was still sifting memories of my time with Operation Washtub when Mike pulled his big Suburban into the Cooper Lake trailhead parking area. We unloaded my gear and I double-checked it for completeness—this was a long hike and I didn't want to run out of anything essential. I had even included military MRE rations as the primary grocery staple, weight-saving taking priority over flavor. I was in pretty good physical condition for a man my age, but had to admit that age was becoming a factor in a lot of my decisions lately. I referred to myself as being in the mature forties—Liz liked to call it the damn-near-fifties.

Last summer's escapades, searching for wrecked airplanes and stray Russians, had toughened me at the time, but a lazy winter and a fat spring had taken their toll. I was definitely not ready for any marathons—except possibly as a spectator at the Seward race.

"You carrying a shotgun for bear?" asked Mike. "I hear they're thick this year."

"Only this," I said, pulling my little snub nosed 38 from its home in the shaft of my specially modified right boot.

"What! You shoot a bear with that and he finds out about it, he'll make you eat that gun. Then he'll eat you!"

"Just kidding," I laughed. "This is my pot meat gun. Grouse and such. I'm carrying the 338 for life insurance." I slipped my old Winchester Model 70 rifle out of its battered case and handed it to Mike. He opened the bolt and probed the chamber with his little finger to make sure the rifle was empty.

"Decent old gun," he said as he examined it. "This the one you've been carrying forever?"

"Seems like forever," I said, "but I haven't found one that suits me better. It hits where it looks, and the target always falls down."

'Except just once,' I thought to myself, recalling a missed shot last summer that cost the life of an innocent woman. I shook my head, trying to cast off a memory that still tended to inflict guilt whenever it recurred.

I loaded the Winchester, closed the bolt over an empty chamber, and dropped a few loose rounds in each of my side pockets, handy for a quick reload if needed.

"Thanks for the lift, Mike, and thanks for saving me 10 miles of walking. If I don't get et' by a bear, I'll drop by the landing on the way home and buy you a beer."

We shook hands and Mike climbed into his rig and made his way back down the mountain. I hoisted my pack and squirmed around until it settled most comfortably on my shoulders, adjusting the belly belt to carry most of the weight. Later I'd be shifting the load to shoulders and back again as I walked, trying to minimize the strain on any one set of muscles.

HOW WE GONNA DO IT?

"The big race is Friday," said Pete. "Thursday'll be all confusion when the cops and city workers start blocking off streets for the start of the race and setting up the finish line. We'll hit the bank just before noon and haul ass outta town through all the commotion."

"Hell, Pete, the cops'll call the State Troopers and the Anchorage police and have the highway blocked at every intersection and road fork north of here. No way we can get clear of this place with only one road out. Unless you got a boat or a plane we don't know about, that don't sound like much of a plan to me." Sam's voice began to fade on his last comment as he realized he had just criticized a plan constructed by a brutish egotist with a hair-trigger temper. To his surprise and relief, Pete's response was a knowing smile rather than the half-expected fist in the gut.

"That's the beauty of it. We ain't gonna try something as stupid as driving outta town. We're gonna hike out on an official Forest Service trail!"

He went to the bed in the corner and pulled a large folded map from beneath the tattered mattress. Spreading it across the table he pointed out the town of Seward.

"We're here. The Exit Glacier is here. The road to Exit Glacier goes on another few miles to a trailhead." His finger traced a line from the trailhead northward through the mountains toward Cooper Landing.

"This is the Resurrection River and a trail alongside it that'll get us to Cooper Lake and the Sterling Highway. That's about a 20-mile hike, but we ain't gonna go all the way for a while. We'll probably make it half-way the first day; then we'll lollygag along, spend some time in good camping places, and come out at the Landing after the heat's off. By then, they'll be watching the border and the airports, and trying to figure how we beat all the roadblocks."

There was silence as Sam and Eddy tried to absorb Pete's unorthodox getaway plan.

"You mean," said Sam, "that instead of crashing outta town, running roadblocks, and getting our asses shot at, we're gonna be picnicking in some moose meadow while the law tears up and down the Kenai looking for us?"

"You got it. How does that sound to you yardbirds?"

"Sounds to me," said Eddy, "like we gotta round up some camping gear pretty quick. Friday's coming fast."

"Yep. You boys better get at it. I still gotta finish this sawed-off."

Pete put next to the last fresh blade in the saw frame, braced the shotgun under his left knee, and began the monotonous "zoop, zoop, zoop", again. He felt that this one item of firepower was necessary for the proper intimidation of the customers and employees of the bank. Sam had only a small 22-automatic pistol, unimpressive to say the least, while Eddy had stolen a cheap Saturday-night-special revolver from under a truck seat. It was in 32-caliber, and only had four rounds in the cylinder.

Pete would have liked a Tommy Gun or an Uzi—he had long envisioned himself walking into a bank and demanding the attention due him by firing a long burst into the ceiling. Since such exotic weaponry was not to be had in Seward—at least, not without raiding the local police station—Pete figured the next best persuader was a sawed-off shotgun. His decision was reinforced by the discovery of a shotgun in the rafters of the cabin after they had taken it over last week.

The forward length of the shotgun barrels suddenly bent back and snapped off, leaving the new muzzle a ragged mess with jagged edges ready to lacerate the hand that carelessly grasped it. Pete studied his work, tried jamming the barrel-end down under his waist band, imagining it concealed under a jacket or coat. No way! The buttstock would jab him beneath the chin. More sawing needed—wood this time. He withdrew it, bringing along shreds of a shirttail, underdrawers, and a square inch of bloody skin, all hanging from the jagged burrs of the roughly cut muzzles.

His roar of profanity sent Sam and Eddy scampering up the dirt road toward the highway, ostensibly seeking camping gear and grub worth stealing, but mostly to avoid becoming collateral damage.

NOT FOR THE FAINTHEARTED

Unlike most of the Forest Service Trails that I had hiked, this one kept pretty well to wooded areas. No steep climbs or alpine country to traverse, just evergreen rain forest and grassy bottoms along streams and rivers. I tried to avoid too much optimism—I had learned long ago that grassy bottoms along streams and rivers often meant boggy bottoms and wet stream crossings. And wooded areas might mean downed trees and formidable root wads blocking the trail just where any detour would send you off a bluff or into a beaver pond.

For the first few miles, the trail was dry, well used, and obviously well maintained by Forest Service crews. I came upon only one blow-down, fairly recent judging by the freshness of the foliage. It was a fairly large spruce, one with insufficient clearance to crawl under and too thick with branches to climb over. Detouring around it only added a few yards to my hike, and was easy enough since previous walkers had pretty well beaten down a trail.

After two hours of hiking with several stops to rest or admire a particularly striking view, I came to the junction of the Russian Lakes and the Resurrection River trails. I took a sharp left onto the Resurrection trail, marked by a small temporary sign warning that the trail was apt to be blocked by downed trees and flooded stream crossings, and was not for the fainthearted.

'Fainthearted? Me?' I thought to myself. 'If an old mountain hand like me can't handle a Forest Service trail designed for summer tourists, he should stay home.'

In the dim recesses of my subconscious, I heard the silken voice of Liz. "It may have been designed for tourists, but not for stupidly reckless, cocky idiots who never take good advice."

Having had such conversations with Liz in the past, I was forced to admit she had sometimes been right. So—I would go ahead and try the trail, but with due caution. I'd be especially careful to evaluate any hairy situations and take the easy way around—if there was one. That resolution made and promptly forgotten, I struck out on the new trail south.

The Resurrection River trail showed much less use than the Russian River trail had shown, and much less maintenance as well. Grass had grown high and overlapped the footpath in places, and devil's club seemed to have been planted in the precise spots where one needed to reach out for balance or support. Then the blow-downs began to show. It must have been a windy winter in this section of the hills; spruce, large and small, had been scattered on the ground like pickup-sticks in some areas, and even an occasional cottonwood had fallen to the winds funneling up or down the valleys.

Some had been chain-sawed through and the trail cleared, others too dangerous to move, still blocked the trail, the clearing crews merely blazing a path around them. Many had been downed after the clearing crew went through, and were untouched.

I had walked the first five miles or so in a couple of hours; during the second two hours, I may have covered a mile. The pack seemed like it was filled with iron cannonballs, the rifle sling was cutting a permanent groove in my shoulder, and the patches of high grass spewed clouds of biting insects as I plowed through them. Just as I was wondering if I were one of the fainthearted after all, a clearly audible grunt, almost like a giant hog, sounded from a clump of thick willow brush directly ahead. At the same instant, the stench of rotting meat wafted in on the faint breeze.

ZEET, ZEET, ZEET

Pete looked down with satisfaction at his handiwork. He had found a carpenter's hammer in a drawer, along with miscellaneous other rusting tools, and had used it to hammer down the sharp burrs and ragged edges that had been left by his inexpert shortening of the shotgun's barrels. The result would have brought tears to the eyes any gunsmith, but it met Pete's standards.

Now, for the buttstock. The only saw available to Pete was the hacksaw with its fine-toothed, well-worn metal-cutting blade. He braced the gun across a chair and under his knee and began sawing off the rear of the stock just behind the grip and triggers. The tiny worn-away teeth of the blade barely scratched the seasoned walnut stock, and their "zeet, zeet, zeet" monoton-ously sang away for ten minutes while creating a mere half-inch cut.

Pete's arm was tiring and his temper frazzling; he thought of the axe on the wood pile behind the cabin, dismissed the idea as impractical— one of his few wise decisions of the week. He resigned himself to an hour of sawing, entertaining himself all the while with thoughts of spending the bank loot on some California or Florida beach.

There came a time when the "zeet, zeet" ended with a splitting sound as the stock separated, leaving a long sharp splinter protruding from the section still attached to the gun. When Pete happily grasped the gun, ready for use at last, he naturally jabbed himself with it—unnaturally, however, he didn't lose his temper. He calmly opened his pocket knife, trimmed off the splinter, and whittled the sharp corners off the grip.

Like a child with a new toy, he cocked the two hammers and waved the weapon around in a threatening manner, visions of cowering civilians and bank clerks in his mind.

Pete had never closely examined the shotgun, except to assure that it was a 12 gauge. It was actually a beautiful arm before he began his alterations—French walnut stock with flamboyant grain and delicate checkering, the trigger guard and receiver finely engraved, the barrels finished in a translucent brown over a complicated mottled pattern, and exquisitely sculpted outside hammers. In tiny letters engraved in the sides of the lock plates were the maker's marks, "J. Purdey & Sons".

A James Purdey-crafted shotgun being worth from $20,000 to $35,000 to collectors and arms aficionados, Peter Paul Peterson had, by his own hand and his gunsmithing skills, converted a work of art into an 85-dollar collection of mangled parts.

GENTLEMEN'S AGREEMENT

I froze. Nothing stirred. The odor of carrion persisted.

There was no doubt in my mind that there was a bear ahead of me, probably lying on an old kill. If the animal even suspected that I had designs on its dinner, it would probably charge—and I might become desert.

'Right now,' I thought, 'that bear's no more sure where I am than I am of where he is. Best not to tell him.'

I backed very slowly and very quietly down the path I had just taken, sliding the rifle off my shoulder to a ready position. The chamber was still empty, but I couldn't load it without the betraying sound of the bolt moving back and forth. Backing up while casting glances behind to keep from tripping and getting the attention of the already alerted bear, I retreated about 50 yards before wetting my feet in a small stream.

I recalled that the stream trickled down from above via a shallow, not-very-steep ravine with only scattered vegetation along its sides. After stepping across it, I made my way up its far side, very slowly and very quietly. I stopped every so often to scan the wood and thickets below for any sign of the bear. My final stop was over a hundred yards above the trail, where I froze; a large brown bear appeared below, standing erect and testing the air. He located me and peered up from the thicket where I had first heard his questioning grunt. The bear and I stared at each other for a matter of 30 seconds or more, neither moving. Finally, we appeared to reach a gentlemen's agreement—if I showed no interest in his dinner, whatever or whoever it might be, he was content to allow me to bypass his dining site. One might call it a compromise—I agreed to let him eat in peace, and he agreed not to rip me limb from limb. He dropped back to all-fours and was swallowed by the brush; I continued my very wide detour around him and his repast and bush-whacked my way back to the main trail.

The unplanned detour had cost me nearly an hour of tight nerves and brush-bucking. After moving another hour down the trail to reduce the likelihood of the bear scenting and becoming interested in my own dinner, I began looking for a decent camp site. I didn't want to camp near the trail—I had seen enough bear tracks along the softer sections to know that bear also preferred it as an easier route than bucking brush through the stream bottoms.

I found another small stream trickling downslope and followed it up until it passed through a small patch of clear ground. It was a little soggy and with no level spots, but probably as good as I was likely to find. There was enough old downed timber that I was easily able to rig a lean-to shelter with my lightweight plastic tarp. By butting the closed side against the bole of a large downed spruce, the open side facing uphill, I would be cuddled against the trunk without danger of rolling down the slope in my sleep.

I found enough old dead limbs to form a fair-sized pile of firewood and built a fire near the open side of the lean-to. It produced little heat but lots of smoke, and soon drove away the man-eating insects that had been feasting on my sweaty hide.

In thinking about my rather short day on the trail, I had to face the fact that I was not in the condition I had thought I was. Not that I was exhausted or really hurting, but I was surely worn down. I wondered if it was because of the stress of the bear encounter as much as physical strain, but decided against that; I had not been afraid of the bear so much as I had dreaded having to kill it.

No doubt a sudden up-close encounter in tall grass would have induced fear and a bucket of adrenalin—the chances of being mauled would have been high. But in the situation that existed, I was sure I could have chambered a round and quickly killed the creature had it become necessary.

It seemed as though I had reached a point in life where killing anything that I couldn't eat, or didn't need the hide, was becoming distasteful to me.

Later in the evening as I lay awaiting sleep, I reexamined those thoughts and considered their validity. The present Ben Hunnicutt claimed that he wouldn't kill a world-record Dall sheep if it appeared in front of him and he didn't need the meat. The Ben Hunnicutt of a year ago had cold bloodedly killed one man, and was about to kill another if someone hadn't done it for him.

'Do you value an animal's life more than that of a man?' I asked myself.

'Well, maybe more than that of some men,' I answered.

'What entitles you be the judge?' No response.

'So you'd kill only those who you personally think deserve killing?'

I had no answer to myself, and a lone wolf off in the hills complained that I was thinking too loud, so rolled over in my bag and sought sleep.

THE PLAN

Sam and Eddy returned late the previous evening in an older Ford half-ton pickup. They patiently cowered while Pete gave them a tongue lashing for bringing in another hot truck. When Pete's invective seemed to have finally been exhausted, Eddy explained their actions while Sam prepared himself for flight if the explanation turned out to be inadequate.

"Dammit!" said Eddy, "We couldn't haul four backpacks fulla gear back here on foot. If there had been a squawk, we'd have been spotted right away. You'd have had to pull off the job by yourself while we were in the cooler trying to explain ourselves."

Since Pete appeared to actually be listening, Sam chimed in. "We went to the Alaska Railroad Station while a train was unloading a herd of tourists. A bunch of college kids stacked their packs along the small boat harbor walk and wandered off taking pictures of everything."

"Yeah," said Eddy, "We picked up the truck right after the owner parked it and took off in the 30-foot Bayliner he'd been towing. We knew he wouldn't be back to look for it until late—maybe even not for a coupla' days— so I hot-wired it and drove it along the docks while Sam scarfed up the best looking of the kid's packs and tossed em in the bed."

"And now we have two trucks to use," said Sam, "One maybe hot and the other not-so-hot for a while."

"OK," said Pete, "I got a use for the other. You done good."

Unused to any sort of compliments from Pete, they glanced carefully at each other. Taking advantage of the mellow mood, Sam turned to Pete.

"We kinda searched through the packs after we left town. Would you believe those kids had stashed away some pretty good booze? I'd have expected pot, but didn't find any."

He went to the truck cab and returned with two bottles of Old Crow and one of Chivas Regal.

Pete confiscated the scotch for his own later use; the bourbon was placed reverently on a shelf until the evening meal of canned chili was disposed of. Then the seals were broken and a party began, of which none of the participants remembered the end.

The following morning, if noon could be referred to as morning, Pete bullied his crew into semi-consciousness.

"This is the last day," he loudly and painfully reminded them, "and we gotta get our shit straight. First, we gotta make up these packs so's every man has got enough gear to get by with for two or three days. Actually, figure on four, but we shouldn't need that much.

"First, the stuff we can all use; cook stove, water bottles, cooking pans, coffee pot…"

"Hey," said Sam, "It's only three or four days—we can handle most anything for that short a time. Let's go as light as we can. We don't need to haul along a stove when we can just build a fire. And why carry canteens or water bottles? Water's heavy and there're plenty of streams and creeks right where we're going. And I can go without coffee for four days if everybody else can."

Soon the gear from all four packs was spread out on the floor of the cabin. Their content was carefully picked over and select items were put into three piles. The piles were augmented by groceries from the cabin's pantry, which had been well-stocked when the trio had broken in and taken possession. The most popular food items were the various canned goods, everybody being familiar with them and knowing that they wouldn't spoil. A typical inventory of any of the three packs would have read something like:

Four cans of peaches; seven candy bars of various chocolate flavors; six cans various sweet soft drinks; six cans Spam, pork and beans, or chili, depending on tastes; a cheap plastic tarp with a hole sliced in the center, poncho-style; a bottle of bug dope; and a book of guaranteed-waterproof matches. There was also a small Boy Scout-style hatchet with leather belt sheath set off to one side, together with a pocket compass.

"Now, about tents," said Pete, "I'm too big to share one, and wouldn't share with either of you anyway—unless you was built different. If you two wanna bunk together, it'll save the weight of one tent."

"Suits me," said Sam, looking dubiously at the mound of stuff before him. Eddy picked through the stolen gear and uncovered three tents. Pete looked over the tents and picked the lightest one for himself. Sam and Eddy chose the next lightest. No one bothered to unroll and check out the mechanics of setting up the tents—after all, a tent is a tent.

"Now," said Pete, "here's how it'll go. Tomorrow at ten, Eddy'll drive the old truck out to the campground beside the beach. Rub everything down to get rid of fingerprints and strip anything else out that could lead back to us. Park it near some expensive motor homes. At ten minutes after, Sam and I'll park the new truck near the entrance."

He looked around for questions, but everyone seemed to follow him so far.

"Eddy, take with you a couple of those red road flares we found in the old truck. And take along a small pile of dry wood. Put the pile of kindling behind the seat under and around the gas tank. Got it?"

Eddy nodded and Pete continued.

"Set the butt ends of the flares under the kindling pile and set both flares off, shut the door, and move out. Don't run or attract attention. Time it so you'll get to us in our truck right at ten-ten." He paused.

"Everybody with me?"

Heads nodded.

"Now if I figured right, we'll get to the bank just about the time the flares burn down to the wood and everything catches fire. We'll park our truck in front of the bank and go in just about the time the fire's reported and police and firemen head that way. We'll get everybody on the floor, I'll hold em while you two clean out the cages and the vault. OK?"

He pulled a green rubberized duffle bag from under his bed.

"We're gonna fill this mother!" he declared, "and never have to take any crap from anybody again." Sam and Eddy privately hoped the "anybody" included Pete.

BEARS VS RAMS

I awoke earlier than I had intended, lay unmoving until my senses had assured me that I was alone in my sparse camp, crawled out of my bag, and built a small fire. Once I had taken care of nature's needs, I returned to the fire and coaxed enough life into it to heat a cup of water to coffee intensity. A spoonful of instant from the Army rations transformed the water to a reasonable near-coffee and thus me to a near-human.

I was sore from the unaccustomed walking, and from climbing over, through, and around the blowdowns. My pack also seemed a good bit heavier than I remembered, but my only physical wounds were those inflicted by voracious flying insects. The inexorable force of gravity, pressing my body against the bole and roots of my supporting tree during the night, had left me in a semi-permanent crouch for the first few minutes of my day. So much for the joys of being a tree-hugger.

Breakfast was GI MRE's, about as dull tasting as their Federal Stock Number, but adequate if one doesn't expect flavor with his breakfast. I took my time packing up for the trail, allowing the stiffness of my newly awakened muscles to subside.

When I dropped back down the slope to the trail below, I was alert for bear, but saw only a fat moose cow and her gawky calf browsing alongside the stream. I knew that if a bear were nearby, it would be interested in the calf—and if it were upwind of the pair, the cow would know it. She appeared at peace with the world, ears forward and shoulder hackles undisturbed, so I felt comfortable when I struck the trail. Upwind was southward, my direction of travel.

Today's portion of the trail was nearer the stream that it followed, and was more open and less impeded by downed trees. It was grassier, however, and more infested with mosquitos and black flies. I finally gave up and dug out my mosquito head net. It was a clumsy thing and a nuisance—hard to see out of and easily thrust awry by the head-high vegetation that sometimes plucked at me. It did, however, keep the bugs out of my face and off my neck, so I forgave it its sins and shortcomings and wore it with a combination of patience and profanity.

The Resurrection River was actually becoming one, the small feeder streams tumbling down from the mountainsides had fattened it from a small creek into a stream with respectable depth and noticeable current. The further downstream I travelled, the healthier it grew.

The way being easier today, I took my time and enjoyed the views of the snow-dappled mountains and of the occasional wildlife that appeared along the trail and on the slopes above. Several small flocks of Dall sheep browsed high in the green meadows between snow patches left over from winter. I could see the inky black dot of a black bear lower on the mountain, below the sheep but working his way up toward them. My binoculars revealed several very young lambs gamboling around near one of the flocks, often out of sight of their usually watchful mothers. This surprised me so I sat down on a log and braced the binocs for a better look. The adults of the flock, mostly ewes and immature rams, were in a bare spot, and were apparently eating or licking up the soil. That easily explained their inattention to the young.

The sheep had found a mineral lick and, after a long winter when such licks were inaccessible due to snow or ice, were making the most of it. The bear, however, was doing a pretty good job of keeping alder thickets and rock outcroppings between itself and its intended lambchop dinner. Perhaps it got too cocky, perhaps a stray breeze carried bear scent to the flock, or perhaps a mama was keeping better watch than it appeared. First, I saw one ewe abruptly straighten, then the entire flock came to attention. A second later the flock dispersed upslope like a double handful of thrown snow.

The sheep scampered up the slope about a hundred yards, then all stopped and peered down at the bear, which had stopped when the sheep fled. The flock began feeding at their new level, ignoring the bear, who immediately began another stalk. This time, the sheep allowed the bear to within 25 yards whereupon it tried a clumsy uphill charge. The sheep almost casually trotted uphill again and renewed their feeding another 25 yards higher. The bear climbed slowly after them, stopped short of the flock, then charged again like a furious bull. On level terrain, a bear can charge at a speed hard to outrun. Downhill, it can cover ground like a freight train. Uphill, not so much.

This time, the sheep moved only a few feet higher, and without any particular alarm. They had the bear's number, and they knew they could elude him at will. They seemed to be patiently waiting for the bear to figure it out also and leave, so they could go back to their salt lick for dessert.

Not wanting to dally too long, I hoisted my pack, slung my rifle, and resumed my journey. At last glimpse, the bear had side-hilled away from the sheep and appeared to be working its way around the mountain to get above them. I'd like to have stayed and watched the drama play out, but was pretty sure that any bear without wings would be unable to out-climb Dall sheep.

FIRE IN THE HOLE!

It was Thursday morning, THE morning, and Pete's gang of three was nervously going about its preparations for the big Seward bank heist. The town was filling up in anticipation of the Mount Marathon race on Friday. Most of the five-man police force was out blocking roads and channeling traffic in preparation for tomorrow's crowds.

At ten o'clock, Eddy drove up to the gate of the campground, peering around for the big motor homes that Pete wanted to threaten with the burning truck. His scanning of the campground distracted him from noticing that the gate was closed by a stout rope, a sign hanging from it stating that the grounds were full.

He eventually noticed when his front grill struck the rope, snapping off the two four-by-four posts and splitting the sign. He also noticed a park caretaker running toward him, shouting, and shaking his fist. Quickly reversing the vehicle, he backed out into the street and banged into a pickup-camper which had been following him into the now-open gateway. He jammed the truck into gear and fled the scene in a panic, wondering if he had screwed up the entire plan. No provision had been made or discussed in the event something went wrong. When Pete dictated a plan, nothing was supposed to go wrong; if it did, it was someone else's fault.

Eddy was never quite sure how he had become a part of Pete Peterson's little group. It first started when Eddy was propped up against the bar in a Fourth Avenue dive in Anchorage, getting the hell slapped out of him.

Eddy never recalled what he had said—he thought it might have had to do with someone's favorite pro-football team. In any case, three burly north slopers—each large enough to have played on a pro-team—were bouncing him around like a beach ball. A big stranger stood back and watched the fun, not with any sympathy for the little guy being mercilessly pummeled, but with the casual interest one might have in an ongoing game of checkers. His interest grew more than casual when one of the slopers bumped into him and spilled his drink.

The bumpee, who turned out to be Pete, spun the bumper around and demanded he buy a replacement. Receiving only a sarcastic laugh in return, Pete enthusiastically waded into the melee. Not content with destroying the trio of slopers, Pete took advantage of the situation to work off his frustrations on anyone else in the bar who made a convenient target.

After having run out of targets, Pete sauntered out of the bar to find Eddy, waiting on the sidewalk to thank him and perhaps to buy him a drink at an intact bar further down the avenue. The yodel of police sirens put an end to their plans, and both spent a little time in the local lockup for D & D. Upon being released, they stuck together and drifted down to Seward where there was no Fourth Avenue, and where they had not yet attained police blotter status.

Eddy made a right turn, went over a block, turned right again, and reverse paralleled the street he had been on before the gate incident. The truck that he had backed into didn't seem to be chasing him, so he decided to hide in plain sight. He drove a few more blocks, turned right again, and made another right back onto the street traffic running past the campground.

Realizing that Pete would be approaching soon to pick him up, he drove to within a hundred yards of the now ropeless gate where aspiring campers were enthusiastically clogging the entry in hopes of a spot for the night. He drove up onto the left shoulder and opened the door. Reaching back into the cramped rear area, he gathered the combustibles into the requisite piles and struck the igniters on the two flares. Since nobody had thought check the flares, only one ignited—part of the striker surface had somehow been torn off the other.

Eddy slammed the door and walked quickly away from the gate and the smoldering truck, searching traffic for Pete and Sam.

LIZ HAS SPOKEN

My day had begun quite nicely, I thought. A pleasant encounter with the lady moose and her calf, and a fascinating sideshow put on by the bear and sheep ballet troupe. I had long ago learned to rate my wilderness days by such incidents. One such made it a good day on the trail; two or more made a great day—one I'd write Liz about. I was composing the letter in my mind when I came to a sudden halt, my day turning sour.

The trail had crossed many feeder streams, most of which were easily fordable without getting too wet. Rather than haul the weight of a pair of hip boots, I had started carrying a couple of rolled up industrial strength plastic trash bags. Weighing only a few ounces, they were quick to step into for a dash across a shallow stream. If they picked up a few punctures, they were readily patched by plastic tape. An easy solution to the misery of marching miles in wet socks and boots.

But now, I was facing a swift glacial stream that actually had a foot bridge over it. Well, part of a bridge anyway. Winter snows or spring floods, or perhaps both, had wrecked the wooden structure. There were still some uprights and stringers loosely connected, most with fast water spilling over them like a mill dam. There were 20 feet of fast water, probably four or five feet deep, to cross. The trash bag expedient wouldn't work very well for this crossing, at least not unless I wanted to pack a couple of bags full of silty water up the trail.

Examination of the skeleton of the bridge suggested that I might crawl across on the remaining framework without getting too wet, but not with a pack and a rifle. And if I tried with pack and rifle and got dumped, this stream was deep and swift enough that I would have to lose all my gear to save myself. To be stranded soaking wet half way between Cooper Landing and Seward, and with no gear, was playing Russian roulette with half the chambers loaded. A long night of strong winds could find me dead of exposure in the morning.

My mind involuntarily went back to one of Liz's more emphatic lectures on wilderness safety during her most recent visit.

"Let's face it, Buster, you're not a teenager anymore—even though you tend to act like one. You don't bounce when you take a fall, you swim like a rock, and you can't whip a bear in a fair fight." As I opened my mouth to object, she had clapped her hand over it and continued.

"You take dumb chances when I'm not around—but I hear about them. I'm FBI, remember—I have informants." I tried again to speak.

"Shuddup! Now I know I can't cure you of all your bad habits, and that's the only kind you seem to have lately. Just do me one favor?" I nodded, half expecting to feel her hand again if I spoke aloud.

"Promise me that when the time comes to make those damn fool decisions, you stop and ask what I would advise. I'm not asking you to take that advice—just consider it!"

I turned to follow the bank of the torrent upstream, hoping to find a wide shallow spot where I could wade across doing the plastic bag bit. The valley bottom here was a vast bog crowded with Volkswagen-sized islands of semi-floating vegetation. I could see that a mile further upstream the ground hardened and cleared. Beyond that point, the stream was gushing down a mountain gorge like a mini-Niagara. Hell, no!

I turned back to the ruins of the bridge, slipped off the pack and rifle, and sat down with my back against a handy log to consider the problem. I even asked myself what Liz would advise. The sun grew warm, the rushing stream furnished a hypnotic background noise, the insects quietly hummed as they attempted to find ways through my head-net and clothing. I fell asleep.

LOADED AND READY

Pete and Sam were puzzled at the knot of traffic near the campground gate. At least it gave them an excuse for stopping and blocking traffic while they looked for Eddy, but Pete was anxious to have the burning truck distraction at the instant they hit the bank. If all was settled down before they could even reach the bank, it wouldn't do them much good.

The sudden "blam, blam, blam!" of Eddy slapping the side of the truck caused Pete to flinch against the accelerator, which caused the truck to lurch forward, which dragged Eddy, who was clutching the right door handle, several yards up the street.

"Dammit, lemme in!" he yelled, running to keep up.

Pete managed to get his foot off the gas long enough for Sam to drag Eddy up onto the front seat.

"I couldn't get into the campground," Eddy gasped, "but it's parked right there on the street. And it's burning."

By this time, they were abreast of the abandoned truck, and it was definitely burning. A conscientious passer-by had jerked the door open to assure that no one was trapped inside. His noble act had burned his hand, which he snatched away from the now-open door, which introduced fresh air and oxygen to the smoldering interior, which fanned the flames into a larger fire, which got hotter yet, which built pressure in the gas tank, which went "whoomp!" and turned the cab into an inferno.

Pete's driver's side window was open, his burly arm hanging out. When the "whoomp!" occurred, the burning truck's window shattered and all the hair on Pete's left arm curled up and blew away. Their truck was still bogged down by the traffic snarl at the gate—Pete's "Gawwdammit!" was nearly lost in the squawk, honk, and blare of horns as he pulled a U-turn without looking and reversed course away from the pandemonium behind.

They stopped on one of the quieter cross streets to settle their minds and get their armament together for the bank invasion ahead. Pete proudly pulled his sawed-off 12 gauge from under the seat and dug in his pocket for a pair of shells.

"This'll tame 'em," he chortled, dropping the big shells into the chambers with an audible "thoomp, thoomp" and snapping the gun closed. "I found some high-powered express loads on a shelf in the cabin, along with a couple of slugs. The shot loads'll do for the bank, and the slugs'll take care of any bear we might meet on the trail". He, of course, was too busy exulting to notice that he had slipped a slug load into the right barrel rather than shot.

Pete could probably not be blamed for thinking that one size fits all—after all, that was true with baseball caps and tube socks. A hunter or a gunsmith might be able to explain certain technical aspects of ordnance which would be of interest to him if he would listen, but Pete had never excelled at listening.

For instance, finely made English shotguns were most often chambered for mild 2 ½ inch shells, possibly because it was assumed that the owner was a sure enough shot that he had no need of a cannon to bring down a pheasant. Also, older guns with those beautifully patterned twist barrels were proof fired only with black powder, not having the strength to be warranted with modern high-pressure smokeless loads. Modern American 2 ¾ inch smokeless shells, such as Pete had loaded would often fit in the chambers of these old guns, but without sufficient room to let the end crimp straighten out properly. This raised internal pressures far beyond the design strength of the barrels.

Sam tugged his 22-automatic out of his pocket and jammed it under his belt. It was fully loaded with seven rounds of 22 Long Rifle ammo, but Sam had never test-fired it, as that was all the cartridges he owned.

Eddy produced the nickel-plated Saturday-night-special that he had found, broke it open and checked the cylinder for loads. Still only four lonely rounds in the five holes, but Eddy had no thought of ever shooting anyone anyhow. Trying to get into the spirit of the occasion however, he snapped it shut Hollywood style, sending his cartridges flying all over the cab. Since one flew out the open window, when he was finally reloaded, he was holding a three-shooter. Shrugging his shoulders, he dropped it into his jacket pocket and nervously contemplated their imminent arrival before the bank.

BREAKFAST PHILOSOPHY

A particularly persistent mosquito woke me by finding entry under my collar and boring a hole into my neck. Evidently, he had been at it for some time—slapping him produced enough blood to attract a vampire.

I must have dozed for nearly two hours and I awoke to the stirrings of hunger, and with no current desire to challenge the roiling waters. 'OK, Liz. What would you have me do now?'

I could swear I heard a soft voice saying, "Just camp here for the night and worry about crossing in the morning." Or maybe I imagined it, because I wanted to just camp here for the night and worry about crossing in the morning.

A good camp on level ground, no shortage of firewood, and with meat in the pot from a curious but foolish grouse which had left the sheltering forest to peck away at a small patch of gravel—my phantom Liz had been right. I'd enjoy the night and think later about crossing the creek. I kept the fire smoky to discourage small biters and bloodsuckers while I savored the dark meaty breast of the spruce grouse and mentally added a page to my Liz letter.

There's nothing like a bright sunny morning after a good night's sleep in the open. I felt ready for anything, but decided to have breakfast and coffee before tackling the creek and its defunct bridge. While waiting for the water to heat, I took up my binoculars and scanned the mountain slopes to the east. A few small bands of Dall sheep dotted the mountain meadows, and a lonely yellowish white spot up in the high rocks revealed itself to be a mountain goat.

'Strange', I thought, 'how sheep manage to stay so white and clean looking through much of the year, while goats almost always looked yellowish and a little dingy.'

In winter, however, it was easy to spot sheep in snow fields because they did show a yellowish tint when compared to the pure whiteness of the snow. I reflected on that fact for a while, and my mind drifted into the thoughtful philosophy that often surfaced when I was alone in the mountains.

'Perhaps everything is like that. Maybe something is good, bad, or indifferent only as compared to something else. Benito Mussolini was good compared to Hitler. He was bad compared to Mother Teresa. The Ford Model T was great in its day, but junk compared to a Cadillac. A Cadillac is crude compared to a Rolls Royce. A hot dog is junk food compared to a filet mignon, but great at a ball park. The Civil War rifled musket was a good weapon, but a club compared to an AR-15, which was junk compared to a Griffin & Howe custom sporting rifle or a James Purdey shotgun.'

'Now,' I conjectured, 'could we transfer this line of thought to morality? I'm not a perfect person; I've done a few things I'm ashamed of. But compared to some people, I'm a saint. Does that mean I'm a good person? Or, compared to a real saint, am I a sunnuvabitch? Are there degrees of goodness or badness, depending, as we used to say in the military, "on the situation and the terrain" and on who you're being compared to?'

'Whoa!', I thought, 'You don't wanna go there. This is a philosophical discussion better carried out with Liz over a bottle of good Moselle wine.'

I forced myself to break camp and head down to the creek looking for a new inspiration.

On arriving, I found that Liz had been right—overnight a miracle had taken place. The creek had dropped by a good two feet during the night, and enough of the bridge structure was exposed that I should have little trouble shuttling myself and my gear across. It only took a few seconds for me to realize what had happened and to mentally kick myself for not foreseeing it.

The stream was fed by melting snowpack and hanging glaciers high in the mountains on either side of the shallow valley that cradled the young river on its way to the sea. As the day warmed, the melt increased, as did the water carried off the mountains by my inconvenient stream. As the sun moved westward and night came, the melt decreased and the stream subsided.

The receding water had revealed sufficient beams and stringers that I was easily able to pick my way across to the far bank. I did so, and was off again toward Seward.

WILD SHOT

As Pete approached the intersection of 4ᵗʰ Street and Adams, preparing to make the turn that would allow him to park near the bank's entrance, he was waved to a stop by a city worker in an orange high-visibility vest.

"Sorry, Sir. This block's one-way until after the race tomorrow. You'll have to go around and come in the other way."

"Hell, I just need a minute in the bank," complained Pete. "Be outta your way in no time."

"Nope. Come in from the other way." said the worker in a matter-of-fact voice as he turned to admonish the following driver who was attempting to drive around the group.

"Dammit!" Pete turned back and drove around several blocks to approach the street from the other direction. He was still able to park in front of the bank, but only on the opposite side of the street. He realized that this could be slightly inconvenient at getaway time. Sirens began to sound back in the neighborhood of the campground and, a few seconds later, unseen fire trucks began whooping from close by and the sound of powerful engines faded northward. Now had to be the time.

The trio unloaded and, in a guiltily casual manner, ambled across the street and into the bank. There were only a half-dozen customers present and no guards in sight when Pete, with some difficulty, dragged the sawed-off shotgun out of his belt and waved it in the air.

"Everybody on the floor! This is a stickup!"

Evidently, in his nervousness, the order came out as a mild request rather than a demand. A few people looked around, but no one complied.

"Dammit! On the deck! We're robbing this bank!"

Most of the customers paid some attention to the second call and looked down at the floor undecidedly as if debating if this was some kind of joke. Pete was finally in the perfect position to live out one of his ambitions. He pointed his mini-shotgun skyward just as an elderly lady standing ahead of him turned around to see what was disturbing her peace.

Pete cocked both barrels and pulled the front trigger. The gun roared almost in her face and a 12-gauge slug went skyward. The recoil sent the gun spinning out of Pete's hand and to the floor.

The person whose face was powder blackened by Pete's shot was one Matilda Murchison, a lady of some heft who had spent 20 years cooking in logging camps in Southeastern Alaska. She was no stranger to guns, nor to stupid inconsiderate oafs like Pete. Matty had developed a subtle technique for fending off those over- enthusiastic loggers whom she chose to fend off.

She swung a wide roundhouse right, catching Pete solidly on the side of the head with an open-handed swat.

"You stupid asshole!" she snapped. "I oughtta stuff that sawed-off up your butt and pull the trigger!" She was about to say more, but then the rain began. Pete's unaimed shot had neatly severed the main pipe of a newly installed sprinkler system of which the bank was quite proud. Water began pouring down from the ceiling, spattering the entire lobby but pouring directly on Matilda and the current target of her wrath.

"This is a holdup," repeated Pete, shaking his ringing head to clear his vision, "and you gotta . . ."

"I 've got better things to do than stand in the wet and watch your half-ass idea of bank robbing," she said. She shoved him aside and strode out the front entrance, leaving wet tracks on the sidewalk as she looked for a place to report a 211 in progress.

Pete stood for a moment with his jaw hanging down, then retrieved the sawed-off and faced his audience.

GOOD COMPANY

Once the delicate crossing was made, I settled down to a steady pace. The trail here was good—much of it through heavy enough timber that the undergrowth was sparse and easily managed. The few blowdowns were easy to circumvent and seldom required brush whacking through devil's club, or the subsequent time-out to try and remove the tiny toxic thorns it left in your skin and clothing.

Despite the slow first day, hampered by the windfalls, and the second day being abbreviated by the destroyed bridge, I was moving along pretty well this third day on the trail. I could see that I wasn't likely to make Seward in time to see the big race unless I stumbled onto a stray canoe or rubber raft, but I had no one to blame but myself. The extra time spent at Cooper Landing, gabbing, and shooting with the gun shop crowd, had been pleasant, and I could always watch next year's Marathon.

Late in the day, I came upon another rushing creek pouring down from the eastern mountains. I found no bridge, intact or otherwise. In this case, however, I was able to walk upstream until I found a wide shallow bend which appeared fordable. I took out my plastic trash bags, tied one over each leg, and cautiously worked my way across the stream. The pressure of the water nearly took my legs from under me several times, and I could imagine Liz watching and shaking her head in despair.

The roiling current had sloshed a quart or two of silty water over the top of the left trash bag and thoroughly wet my trousers and boot. I decided it was time to set up camp and dry myself before water completely soaked the leather of the boot.

The fire, open and hot for drying my gear, was comforting, the field rations tasted better, and a breeze kept the bugs at bay. The only sour spot of the evening was a touch of loneliness. This was taken care of by a family of five river otters, playing and chittering to each other as they made their exuberant way along the river bank. Their antics, diving, twisting, turning, chasing each other, were like small children taking over their playground during recess. They were good company, and I watched them with pleasure until they worked their way upstream and out of sight.

Chalking up another good day in the woods, and another paragraph in my mental letter to Liz, I lay in the receding sun and lazed away the remainder of the day.

THE HEIST

Sam and Eddy had taken up places near the half-door to the cashiers' area. They waited expectantly for Pete to open the ball, then stood in awkward confusion while the Pete and Matilda show played out. Pete's subsequent glare at them was all the incentive they needed to send them scurrying around to the tellers' territory and putting the tellers, who still weren't sure what was happening, on the floor.

Sam was carrying the big green duffle bag, holding it open while Eddy pitched in whatever greenbacks were evident in the drawers and on the counters.

"The vault; hit the damn vault!" shouted Pete from his place on the opposite side of the counters. Sam reacted quickly, moving to the rear and waving his 22 threateningly at an employee who had finally made a move to close the yawning door of the main vault. The employee wisely backed away and made room for Sam to check the interior.

"Eddy!" he shouted, "Bring the bag. This damn thing is loaded!" When Eddy arrived, both stood transfixed for a few seconds, gazing at the bundles of fresh bills lining the shelves inside After a few seconds of wonderment that any part of Pete's plan was actually going as advertised, they began stuffing money into the big duffle bag.

Natascha Flannigan liked to work alone and in the quiet. As one of the bank's more efficient book keepers, she was allowed to earn her hours cranking a manually operated Burroughs calculating machine in a small office on the second floor of the bank building. Natascha was somewhat annoyed when, in the midst of a relatively complicated juxtaposition of figures, there was a muffled thud from below instantly followed by a more localized splintering sound five feet from her desk.

Now in her sixties, Tasch, as she was called locally, had lived quite an interesting life, some of it in rooms above various saloons and honkytonks in various mining and fishing towns throughout Alaska and Canada. She was no stranger to unexpected gunfire or to the intrusion of random bullets into her personal space. In most cases, it merely meant an over-exuberant miner or trapper letting off steam.

Since, as far as she knew, no alcohol consumption or partying took place in the bank lobby below, the only other explanation for the slug through her floor (and probably her ceiling) had to be some sort of robbery attempt. Sighing at the interruption of the tedious but— to her— fascinating chore, Natascha picked up the phone and called her friend Mabel at Police Dispatch.

"Hi, Mabe, this is Tasch; I think somebody's trying to rob the First National—y'all might wanna look into it." She put down the phone and went back to her calculator.

BEACH BUM

I slept late the following morning, reluctant to leave the warmth of my sleeping bag. As long as I knew I was going to miss the race, there was no particular reason to hurry anywhere. The river was increasing in size as I followed it toward salt water, and there was a broader flood plain and deeper channels. The feeder streams were fewer, smaller, and more easily forded, so I took my time about breaking camp and meandered southward at a leisurely pace. By now, my pack was a good bit lighter and my previously unworked muscles had adapted to the trail.

The only real impediments were the low boggy spots that harbored squadrons of insects, and the patches of high grass that prevented a hiker from seeing a bear until he could smell its breath. There were enough bear tracks on the trail to make the latter a matter of concern, so slow and cautious were my watchwords for the day.

In keeping with my recent change to a take-your-sweet-time mode, I decided to make camp early in the afternoon and enjoy the sun on a nearby gravel bar that jutted out into the river at a sharp bend. The bar had been swept clean of vegetation during the last spring flood and there was a steady breeze which brushed away the hungry insects emerging from the tall shore grass.

I was tempted to pitch camp on the bar itself, but rejected the idea after checking the water level. A six- inch rise of water would have me wading or swimming ashore trying to carry most of the camp with me. I settled for putting the tarp over the gravel, peeling off my shirt and trousers, and imitating a California sun worshiper.

I'd take time to set up camp ashore after the sun faded or the breeze became cool.

THE GETAWAY

"C'mon, get the lead out!" Pete shouted toward the back room. "We ain't got all day!" No water had reached the vault area yet, but the tide was rising in the main lobby as the shot-up pipe continued to gush forth generous quantities of cold mountain water. To cover the entrance, Pete was forced to stand near the cataract, thus soaking his feet and absorbing gallons of the freezing spatter.

Those patrons who were still prone were becoming uncomfortably cold and wet—finally one exasperated gentleman said, "The hell with it. Go ahead and shoot, but I ain't gonna lie here and get pneumonia while you guys screw around." He stood, shook his soaking trouser legs away from his shivering skin, and leaned against the tellers' counter. The remaining customers, hearing no gunshots, stood also. Pete, as cold and wet as any of them, said nothing, but kept the half-loaded shotgun pointed at their end of the room.

Finally Eddy and Sam emerged from the tellers' area waving their pistols right and left and carrying the green duffle bag between them. Pete's eyes popped when he saw the obviously stuffed bag.

"Was it like I said?"

"Hell, yes!" Sam responded, a beatific smile practically splitting his face in two.

"Damn straight!" said Eddy.

"Then, let's go." Turning to the customers, all of whom were standing now, Pete looked as threatening as he could. "You all stay put for ten minutes. Anybody leaves or makes a phone call, I'm coming back and blow your guts out! You people in the back hear that?" he called over the counters.

"Oh, yes Sir," responded a woman in the vicinity of the vault as she picked up a phone and began punching in 911.

The trio of desperados ran from the building, two carrying the green bag between them, heading for the truck parked across the street. Since the strip of street had been made one-way, about twice the normal traffic was moving past the bank—traffic that the trio was forced to wait for before crossing to the parked pickup. Just before Pete was about to explode with rage, and his companions with nervous fear, a typically polite local housewife stopped her Jeep Cherokee and waved them across the street. Eddy smiled a thanks-a-lot, and they trotted across and threw the bag into the bed of the truck alongside their trail packs. Pete and Sam climbed into the bed also and lay down beside the packs and the bag of loot.

Everything was quiet for a matter of ten seconds or so before Eddy hopped out of the cab and frantically asked, "Where are the damn keys?" There was another ten seconds of silence before Pete abruptly sat up, fished around in his water-soaked pockets, and came up with them. Back in the cab, Eddy slapped the keys into the ignition and ground away on the starter. Having already gotten its initial shot of gas when Eddy first pumped the accelerator to start it, the somewhat tired engine choked on its second shot and flooded itself.

Eddy knew the secret of starting a flooded engine—you floor the accelerator and crank the engine until the excess fuel is sucked through the system and the engine starts normally. This, of course, took another 30 seconds, during which all three were rigid with tension and Eddy suddenly felt a real need to find a bathroom. When the engine finally started and the truck with its larcenous load moved away from the curb, a full two minutes had been wasted since their emergence from the bank. The two minutes were sufficient for the two police vehicles which had been involved in untangling the campground traffic jam to be alerted and sent screaming downtown toward the bank.

The alert had specifically been for three bank robbers, led by a really big guy, fleeing in an older model pickup truck. Thus, both police vehicles ignored and blew by a pickup sedately putt-putting up the road, and being driven by a wiry little guy in an otherwise empty cab.

NATURE DOESN'T CARE

I managed to fall asleep during my sun bathing and didn't come alive until a sprinkle of cold rain shocked me awake. The sky had been mostly cloudless when I dozed off, but somehow a mischievous semi-dark cloud had sneaked through the mountains, obscured the warming sun, and spattered me with what felt like liquid ice. I hurried ashore and took shelter under some of the spruce that bordered the trail. When finally warm, and in mostly dry clothing, I pitched camp under the trees, muttering under my breath about the unfairness of luring a man into a state of half nakedness under a warm sun, then pouring cold water on him.

When I finally had a comfortable camp set up and a good fire going, I felt better—enough better, in fact, to kick myself for taking the tricks of nature personally.

After all, I had enjoyed ideal weather for the first days of my trip. A set-back was overdue.

When first introduced to Alaska, I had been told by a new friend that Alaska wasn't really out to get anyone; nature is what she is, and she doesn't really give a damn one way or the other whether you're happy, miserable, or dead. If you want to get along, you just try to be ready for whatever she can throw at you.

Back to philosophy again! Maybe I should write all these deep thoughts down and impress Liz with my wisdom when she visited in a few weeks.

'Yeah,' I thought, 'and how does that usually work out for you?'

I had to laugh at myself, recalling how some of our debates ended. Usually, Liz and I were in agreement on issues of right, wrong, and morality in general, and whether or not a particular individual should have his teeth kicked out. Once in a while, though, she'd come at me from a mental or moral angle that I had never considered, and would succeed in making me feel like an idiot.

I had been known to stretch a law or two. At least one such stretch had cost an evil man his life; others were mostly for convenience—usually, my convenience. A good example might be the spruce grouse which had recently found its way into my cooking pot. Grouse were not yet in season, as I well knew. However, there was a clause in Alaska's book of game laws which said in effect, "Nothing herein shall be construed to prevent a person from taking fish or game for food in circumstances of need." I had long ago concluded that hunger was a form of "need", and conducted myself accordingly. Liz chided me for this reasoning, but she seemed to enjoy the occasional salmon fillet or grouse breast that it provided.

This had been a short day, and mostly an enjoyable one; I'd turn in early, get a good night's sleep, and probably get into Seward in time to look up the Brandt family and help with the celebration for whomever had won the Marathon.

The wolf that had complained to me several nights ago seemed to have found company; I was serenaded by a barber-shop quartet, a complete family judging by the variety of squeals and howls that saturated the air. Much nearer this time, I thought—I hoped to see one somewhere along the trail, but wolves were not generally seen unless they wanted to be. The music faded and my sleeping bag was calling.

HIT THE TRAIL

As the truck approached the Exit Glacier turnoff from the main road, Eddy took a quick look fore and aft—no vehicles in sight, he veered left onto the dirt and gravel road and drove at a moderate pace to minimize dust and undue attention. He drove past a turnoff leading to the left and down to the glacier, kept straight another few miles, and stopped as he came to the Resurrection River trailhead.

The two who had been lying in the bed of the truck alighted, rubbing bruises and accusing Eddy of deliberately hitting every rut and washboard he saw. Their accusations were not altogether without merit, but Eddy managed a regretful apology while congratulating himself on evening up some old scores against Pete. Poor Sam was collateral damage, and would just have to live with it.

After they had taken the camp gear and the green duffle out of the truck bed, Pete had them wipe down every surface on the vehicle that it was possible to touch.

"Eddy," he said, "drive back to where the trees front the road. Pick a spot with solid ground and get a running start; ram this rig as far up into the woods as she'll go. Sam and I will get some of the bushes you knock over and wipe out your tracks."

Eddy found a likely spot about a quarter-mile back down the road where the right-side ditch was shallow. He backed up another 50 yards, stopped, and took a run at the ditch and into the wooded area behind it. Aside from the fact that he bounced off the roof of the cab several times, the maneuver was successful; the truck settled into a soft depression well off the road and the surrounding brush was thick enough that, with a bit of encouragement, it concealed the vehicle.

It took another ten minutes to brush away most of the tracks and stomp the ditch back into shape. The trio moved themselves and their possessions out of view of the road and began the transformation into a band of happy hikers.

Their first move was to unzip the green duffle bag and admire the fruits of their labor. Bundles of fresh banknotes filled the green bag—none of the three could resist stirring through them, washing their hands in the fortune of bills. Eddy was the first to break the spell.

"Hey, shouldn't we be getting the hell outta here?"

"You're right," said Pete. "Let's get these packs on and get up the trail a mile or so. We can count this stuff later in camp."

Getting the packs on was no simple chore. They had been randomly filled on the cabin floor, canned goods and camp gear tossed in wherever it would fit. None of them had tried one on or attempted to adjust the straps and belts to fit him. As a result, Pete found himself immobilized by two shoulder straps that he couldn't get his shoulders through, while Eddy's pack hung down around his butt like a bomber pilot's parachute. Sam, a lucky medium, got saddled up quickly enough, but felt the sharp rim of every can digging into his back and kidneys.

In the midst of the complaints and profanity, Pete roared, "Knock it off! We gotta get going on this trail and put up a camp far enough along that nobody thinks of checking us out. Now how are we gonna carry the money bag?"

Due to their propensity to grab for canned goods, about the heaviest groceries available, all the packs weighed 40 to 50 pounds—a bone-straining load for men unaccustomed to carrying their living on their backs. The money bag, filled to overflowing with their good fortune, weighed nearly another 45.

Their solution, which they soon realized would have to be temporary, was to carry the duffle between two of them, the two also carrying their own backpacks. They set off up the trail, the river on their left, and Pete leading. Sam and Eddy struggled along behind, the bag swinging between them, one or the other continually getting forced off the narrow trail and into mud or clumps of tall grass and brush.

After an hour and a half of plodding, sometimes staggering, always cursing, Pete spied a narrow trail leading to a small camping area several hundred yards off the main trail. It was classed as a primitive camp on the

Forest Service map, and consisted mostly of a fire pit and grate in a cleared area, several well-used tent sites, and a grove of birch saplings.

"We'll camp here for tonight and get our shit squared away." he announced, an order which drew instant approval from his troops.

Sam and Eddy dug out the tent they planned to share and looked it over. Baffled, they separated the light mountain cloth from the thin rods and framing which had been threaded through the various loops and sleeves of the tent. Unfortunately for them, the prepositioned hardware had been located so that when clipped together, the tent was almost self-erecting. Now, with the fabric wadded up in one pile and the framework stacked alongside, they had no idea how the tent went together.

Pete had better luck—his tent was a more conventional type. It was missing its stakes and poles, however, so Pete was required to scavenge the nearby forest and cut substitutes with the little hatchet he had brought along.

Midway through the founding of Pete City, hunger pangs began to gnaw at its founders. Sam stopped puzzling over the tentage and suggested a fire and a meal would be in order. Instant agreement was furnished by his companions, and three cans were selected from the commissary. Sam finally located the matches, waterproof matches in an olive drab matchbook, obviously GI surplus.

Eddy gathered wood, built a little tee-pee of twigs, and tore a match from the book. He struck the match, and held the match to the twigs, sheltering it from the breeze with the hand holding the matchbook. The breeze blew the flame away from the twigs and to the matchbook, which immediately flared into a burst of flame and scorched Eddy's fingers.

Eddy flung the burning matchbook away, shaking his left hand and cursing in pain. The matchbook being the only source of fire they had, Pete roundly berated Eddy, who took it in guilty silence.

"Wait a minute," said Sam, "I think I threw a Bic lighter into one of the packs,"

All hands set to searching the packs, Sam finally coming up with the Bic in a side pocket of Pete's pack. Using the Bic, the twigs were finally set afire, and wood added until the group sat around a bright warming campfire.

Pete shoved a large can of chili near the flames, while Eddy and Sam decided on a Dinty Moore beef stew each.

NEIGHBORS

I was nodding by my fire, wondering if I should sack in early, or if that would merely cause me to wake in the small hours and spend the next two hours seeking sleep again.

A nearby explosion abruptly jerked me back into the world. It didn't sound like a normal gunshot—more of a dull "whump" than a sharp report. I sat listening for any explanatory sounds, and was rewarded by the faint clamor of angry voices from downstream. I debated the wisdom of going out to investigate—how smart would it be to stumble into a camp of drunks who may have already fired off some kind of a shot, accidently or on purpose?

I had decided to ignore the report and mind my own business (I could hear Liz saying "attaboy" over my shoulder) when a second report sounded and the voices got louder yet. I felt that I had to go and check the situation out—someone might need help or medical aid. I got up, slipped on my light jacket, slung my rifle, and headed in the direction of the uproar. (I imagined I could hear Liz again, "Mind your own business, Stupid.")

I decided to carry the rifle in a more ready position, and to load the chamber, to which Liz would have begrudgingly said, "That's better, but be careful!".

The camp turned out to be only a few hundred yards downstream and up away from the trail by a hundred yards or so. I approached from the river and in plain view.

"Hello, the camp! Anything wrong I can help with?"

Three men froze in place, their faces showing various degrees of consternation. The men were in assorted sizes, one very large, one medium, the third smaller and wiry. The large man had his left sleeve rolled up and his arm appeared to have been severely sunburned. The two smaller men appeared to have blood spatters on their arms and faces. I saw no long guns in the camp.

"I heard shots—anybody hurt?"

The big man spoke up.

"We were heating up cans of stuff for supper and a couple of the cans blew up. Musta been spoiled, or something. Nobody hurt—scared the shit outta us, though."

I saw the remains of a can on the ground before me and picked it up. It was split open and missing most of what appeared to have been beef stew. I could see that what had appeared to be blood was actually a wide distribution of uncooked stew.

"Well," I said, trying not to laugh aloud, "you know, a lot of these cans have weak spots in the seams. You heat em too hot, the moisture inside boils, builds pressure, and they burst. I generally put the can in a pot of water and heat the whole thing. The can can't get hotter than the water around it, so you're safe."

"Or," I added, "you can open the can and heat the contents in an open pan."

Although the trio was listening intently, I got the impression that they were extremely nervous about my being in their camp. I noticed their eyes dropping often to the rifle that I still had in hand, though the muzzle pointed away from their camp.

"Appreciate the advice," said the big man. "We'll open the cans and heat 'em that way from now on." He turned away, obviously dismissing me from their camp.

I moved back to my own, watching carefully to see if I was followed. There was something hinky about the group, and I didn't trust their intentions. A very odd trio to be recreationally camping, and they didn't seem to know their butts from third base about camp cooking. And they had looked too hard and too long at my Winchester. I unloaded the chamber for safety and went about settling in for the night.

LIFE WITHOUT A CAN OPENER

Pete picked up the only unexploded can of the three. It was severely bulged, and there was no doubt that it would have burst also if left in the heat another few minutes.

"OK," he said, "looks like we gotta open 'em first. Anybody see a pan in all this camping stuff?"

"I saw one," said Sam, "but it was part of the stuff we left behind to make the packs lighter."

Pete glowered. "OK, geniuses, now we gotta eat it right outta the cans, I guess. Who's got the can opener?" Two faces stared back at him blankly.

"Nobody remembered to bring a goddam can opener? Serve you all right if you starve. What the hell good are you anyway?"

Eddy began to get a little tight around the mouth.

"I'll tell you what good we are, Pete. We got that for you while you were taking a cold shower and fussing with that old biddy in the bank!" He pointed to the green duffle bag. "Maybe we oughtta split it right now and go our ways."

Pete had never been accused of being a keen student of human nature, but he somehow surmised that his relations with his cohorts were not quite what they should be.

"Aw, don't get your bowels in an uproar, Eddy. We'll all feel better after we get something in our stomachs. I'll open the damn cans."

He selected a can of pork and beans from a pack and retrieved the hatchet. Holding the can firmly against a flat rock, he pressed a sharp corner of the hatchet blade against the top of the, near the rim.

"Give it a rap with one of them rocks," he instructed Sam. Sam obediently chose a grapefruit-sized rock and struck the blunt end of the hatchet a gingerly blow. A quarter-inch cut opened in the can top and a bit of juice dribbled out.

"Hit it harder. We gotta work our way around the top so's to peel it back."

Ever ready to please, Sam gave the hatchet a solid whack with the rock. A third of the top was sliced inward, the pressure blew a wad of pork fat and beans straight into Pete's face and eyes, and Pete hurled the can into the woods.

"Goddammit, there's gotta be a way. Here, let's try with my knife." He took a pocket knife from his pocket, opened it, and grabbed another can of beans.

"Sam, hold a can down and I'll punch around the top with the knife."

Sam warily did so, keeping his fingers well clear of the top rim. Pete put the knife point against the lid and bumped it cautiously with the hatchet. A cut the width of the blade appeared with no visible side effects, so Pete shifted the point of the blade slightly and lengthened the cut. The process was repeated thirty or forty times until the lid was held by only an inch of metal. Eddy enthusiastically grabbed the opened can, bent the lid back for use as a handle, and placed it on the grate above the fire.

The procedure was repeated until fingers were sore and three cans were heating over the fire. When they seemed hot enough, their owners wadded up handkerchiefs to grip the lids and quickly moved them over to a level spot back from the fire. There was a period of stony silence when all three realized that there were no eating tools at hand. Pete had the knife, but soon realized that spearing individual beans floating in pork fat was not practical.

Neither was their solution to the problem, but it was the only one they had. When the cans had sufficiently cooled to be both handleable and edible, they were tipped up and the drinkable portion of the contents sucked down famished throats. The more solid chunks were fished out by fingers and wiped into equally greedy mouths. This being a tiresome way to eat, Pete took his knife afterward and laboriously whittled out a crude spoon and a clumsy two-pronged fork. The knife being well-dulled by now, he loaned it to his companions to create their own tools.

By this time, the stranger who had visited their camp had been gone nearly two hours. Pete was now having disturbing thoughts concerning their visitor, but none of the three could put their finger on anything odd or suspicious. There was no indication that he suspected them of anything other than ignorance—except that his rifle seemed always at the near-ready position. True, the green bag had been in plain view, but it appeared as normal camping gear. The guy was friendly enough, and didn't seem. . . Wait a minute. The guy had no pack, so he must be camped close by. Close enough to hear the cans explode anyway. Maybe they should set out a guard tonight. Oh, hell—he was only one guy.

In the morning when Pete, Sam, and Eddy crawled painfully out of their sleeping bags, they immediately set about starting a warming fire. Eddy and Sam collected kindling and dead limbs, while Pete carefully arranged them in a pattern which would theoretically produce a quick hot fire in only minutes. All were sore from the night on the hard earth, all were shivering from the cold which had seeped up and into their bones from that earth, and all were ravenously hungry.

Pete made several attempts to ignite some of the smaller fire fodder and wasn't able to produce the slightest glow.

"We need some paper or something to get this going," he muttered, trying the Bic lighter again with no result. "Find some."

A quick search revealed nothing usable; finally, Eddy came up with a possible substitute.

"Hey, how about a few bills from the bank money?" Disregarding the incredulous looks from his partners, he explained.

"Hell, we figured there might be over two hundred grand in the bag—right now, it's sure worth a hundred bucks to me to get fed and warm." The others looked at him more approvingly.

"Get two or three," Pete ordered, "We'll try it."

Eddy went to the green bag and fished out three fifty-dollar bills which he passed on to Pete, who fanned the bills out and applied the Bic. A feeble flame issued from the nozzle, which Pete quickly applied to the bills.

"This ain't right," he said, "These bills don't wanna burn worth a damn." The bills did take fire, but with more smoldering than flaming. He applied the Bic to several points, trying to generate enough flame to start the twigs burning. The Bic's flame subsided to a small blue ball the size of a pea, then completely disappeared. The bills displayed small scorched spots that smoldered for a few seconds before fading away.

"Hey, there's that guy from yesterday—maybe he's got matches." Sam pointed toward the main trail where a figure was trudging southward toward Seward.

"Well, get going. Ask him," said Pete, shoving Sam in the direction of the lone hiker.

No Good Deed

I woke earlier than normal, still a bit itchy about my neighboring campers. They were obviously not hunters, no rifles or shotguns in evidence and seasons were closed. They didn't appear to be people who enjoyed the outdoors, and their camp gear certainly didn't indicate any skills in that direction. My instincts told me they were on the run from something, but I had no idea what.

I decided to give them a wide berth and to report them to the Forest Service people when I reached Seward. 'And,' I told myself, 'I'd better be on the way if I don't want to waste another day.'

I was just getting up to stride on the trail toward Seward when a shout interrupted my thoughts. I saw the middle-sized guy from the clown camp trotting toward me.

"Our Bic lighter ran outta gas and we got no fire this morning. Wondered if you have any matches to spare."

I silently slipped out of my pack, rummaged through the side pockets, and handed him two packs of GI waterproof matches. He took them, relief showing in his eyes, started to turn back to his camp, and hesitated.

"Looks like you're heading in to Seward—probably be there today. You won't need a can opener anymore—we'd buy it if you had one to sell." He held out a fifty-dollar bill which appeared fresh from the mint. I stared at the bill; it was odd in that it had never been folded.

"I didn't bring a regular opener on this trip," I said, "Ate mostly dry rations and candy bars. I'll let you have this, though." I removed a slender chain from around my neck, snapped it open, and slipped off the GI P-38 can opener that rode beside my military dog tag.

The P-38 is a small tab of hardened steel a little over an inch long and a quarter- inch wide having a sharp folding hook hinged to lie flat. They were issued with canned field rations, and have been carried on the dog tag chains of nearly every field soldier since WW2.

There are many guesses as to why it was called P-38—it was never officially designated as such, but some soldier somewhere named it, and the name stuck.

The man looked at the quarter-sized device with confusion.

"How'n hell could you open a can with this damn thing? You gotta be kidding."

Judging by their performance last evening, I could believe that the trio would never figure it out, so I took pity on them.

"Let's go up to your camp and get a can. I'll show you how it works."

He hesitated until I started walking, then reluctantly followed along. As we got close, he shouted a little too loudly, "Hey, he gave us a can opener, but he's gotta show us how it works!"

There was a little scuffling around before I got there, but the two other campers were waiting patiently when we arrived at the dead campfire.

"This is the best I can do for you for opening cans," I said to the largest, obviously the leader of the trio. Picking up a loose can from among the gear scattered about the camp, I gathered the men in close, opened the hinged spur, hooked it on the rim of the can, and twisted the shank until the sharpened spur bit into the can.

"Now," I said, "you just rock it and pull it around the rim until you have it where you want." I finished the cut, thereby opening a can of tomato soup which mostly spilled out onto the ground.

"I'll be damn," said the big man, "An opener the size of a quarter that really works." He shook his head in wonderment "Now we need a fire." He took the matches and, after using several, finally got a few twigs glowing. His partners were busily opening cans with an enthusiasm which made me sure they hadn't eaten since last evening's debacle. While they were preparing their unappetizing breakfasts, I looked around their camp. It appeared that neither of the tents had been erected—that the sleepers had merely rolled up in the fabric and spent the night warming the gravel beneath them. I could guess from my own past experiences that there was not much sleeping done.

The big green duffle bag was not in evidence, although nothing else had changed. My rifle was still slung over my shoulder, and my pack left down by the main trail. As I stood to leave, the big man blocked me.

"Hey, I gotta question. You seem like you been in this country for a while—we been hearing wolves at night. Are they dangerous? I heard some tree huggers say they never attack humans. That seem right to you?"

"Well," I said thoughtfully, "that's what a lotta folks say. Of course, people disappear once in a while in wolf country, and there's no way of knowing what happened to them. But I don't recall anybody reporting to the authorities that he had been killed and eaten by a wolf."

I could see them mulling my last statement over in their minds, trying to figure what it said. The big man spoke up again.

"Another question, just out of curiosity, what are you doing poking around in the woods hereabouts?"

"Heading to Seward to watch the big race," I answered truthfully, "but I'm a day late."

"Yeah," he said, "Us too, but we just decided to lollygag around here for a few days, then show up in town after the crowd has gone."

I knew this was a lie—there had been no sign of anyone on the trail ahead of me, and their camp was certainly not the camp of people who had been three or four days in the wilderness.

I tried to push by him but he easily blocked me. As I turned to evade him, the smaller guy poked me in the middle with a nickel-plated revolver.

"Gimme the rifle," said the big man.

I complied—somehow, it seemed the thing to do at the time.

GOES UNPUNISHED

As Eddy held the man at pistol-point, Sam fished in his pocket for his wallet, handed it to Pete. Pete gave it a quick search and seemed disappointed.

"Looks like he's a retired soldier, Alaska driver's license, all the usual crap, no credit cards, a hundred bucks in twenties." He stuffed the wallet back in the guy's pocket.

"Look, Benjamin, we don't like people hanging around spying on us. Whaddaya looking for?"

"Call me Ben," the guy said, "And I was down on the trail heading toward town. How could I be spying on you?"

Pete searched his mind for an answer—none surfaced.

"You camped close to us and you keep showing up here—gotta be some reason why. I wanna know it."

The man who called himself Ben chuckled to himself and sat down on a nearby log.

"When I heard your cans blow up yesterday, I came over here to see if you needed help. When I was leaving this morning, you stopped me and asked me to come to your camp. How do you call that spying? Let me have my rifle back and I'll get out of your hair for good—you guys can get back to trying to live out here with no fire, no tents, and no idea what you're doing."

Pete, who had been on the edge of doing just that, balked at the implied insult.

"You smell like a cop to me—probably some kinda Forest Service cop that wants to write us a ticket for pissing on the ground."

Ben said, "You can piss anywhere you want, but right now, you're pissing me off. I can appreciate honest caution from somebody that's probably bent a few rules along the way, but holding a person who tried to help you at gunpoint is asking for trouble."

"Hey," said Pete, getting down into Ben's face, "you ain't in a good place to tell me how to run my crew—and it looks to me like you're the one in trouble." He pushed Ben backwards off the log and pinned him down with the muzzle of the rifle.

"Don't let me hear no more crap outta you." He turned to Sam. "Sam, tie his hands! And check that thing around his neck."

Sam and Eddy looked worriedly at each other. They had seen Pete talk himself into a fit of anger before, and the outcome had always ranged from complicated to disastrous.

Sam took the dog tag from Ben's neck and read it to Pete.

"It says:

Hunnicutt, Benjamin T.
O 2021765
T-65 O
Protestant

"What the hell does all that mean?" asked Pete.

"It's my name, Army serial number, date of last tetanus shot, blood type, and religion," said Ben, "in case I became a casualty."

Eddy returned the dog tag chain to the man's neck.

"Hell," he said, "Not a cop, anyway. Let him go and just keep all his ammo. He can't cause any trouble that way. Keep the rifle too, if you like it."

"No, Eddy. We gotta make sure he doesn't get to Seward and report us. They'd figure out what we're trying to do and maybe send State Trooper helicopters after us."

"Then whadda we do with him?" asked Sam. Pete stared at him in stony-faced silence.

"No," said Eddy, "I didn't sign on for no killing. Plus, bank robbing is a federal crime. If we kill anybody, the Feds still have a death penalty, even if Alaska don't."

ALL TIED UP

When I heard them worry about being reported, I recalled the factory-new fifty-dollar bill I had been offered. I pretty well knew now that the trio had pulled off some kind of robbery in Seward and were on the run. What I didn't know was to keep my big mouth shut and not antagonize Pete, the obvious leader. The smaller one that they called Eddy was probably the one with the most common sense, though his size and his very forgettable face meant you could lose him in a crowd of five.

But he could read his boss better than I, and I resolved to key off of him when dealing with Pete. Sam, the middle sized one, spent five minutes scrounging around for a length of rope, finally located one hanging on a loop on one of the tents, and began to bind my hands.

I took particular notice of the rope, and was gratified to see that it was relatively stiff braided nylon about the size of clothesline rope. I held my hands low in front of me so it was more convenient for him to make the final knot on top; he obliged by doing so. I also held them crossed with palms facing to opposite sides, which didn't seem to concern Sam a bit. He cinched the knot tight and stood me up facing Pete.

I had listened to the conversation between the other two and understood its implication.

I still had my ace in the hole—the little 38-revolver nestled in its pocket in my right boot. I'd hesitated to pull it because Pete was obviously not completely rational in his thinking. If I caught them cold with no arms handy, a reasonable person would give up and take his chances. Pete would do something stupid and start a fire-fight that would leave people dead—possibly including me. As long as there was a reasonable chance of escape, I'd rather not have to shoot anyone.

But if Pete had his way, I might have to revert to the little Smith & Wesson, and Pete would be the first to go.

And No Place To Go

Pete was thinking about the new factor that had just been introduced into his planning—the death penalty. While not a deep thinker, he guessed that if they were caught for robbing the bank and a corpse showed up somewhere, somebody would probably make a connection. And there were two men here who would put the blame square on him, even though he did it for their own good.

'Well,' he thought to himself,' they'll probably have to be taken care of later anyway. But for now, I can walk around the problem.'

"Guys, we won't kill him. We'll just tie him up here so he can't get loose for four or five days, and by then we'll be long gone."

He saw the questions in their eyes and continued.

"Man can live a week without food, easy; we'll leave water within reach. Somebody'll likely come along the trail, see him, and cut him loose. And if he does die, we didn't do it. Maybe a bear or something will come along and clean up things up for us."

Pete could see that Sam and Eddy were doubtful, so he changed the subject by distracting them with other problems.

"Go get his pack from the trail. Then break down all the packs and gear. Make up new ones with stuff we need. Get the green bag outta the brush. Let's get ready to move up the trail toward Cooper Landing."

He looked over at Ben with a hint of amusement.

"Sam, take this guy over to that little grove of birch trees. Untie him, wrap his arms around the trunk of one of em and tie his hands on the other side. If he wants to get loose, he can uproot the damn tree or eat through it like a beaver. And bring any cans or anything else that'll hold water, fill 'em up and leave 'em within his reach."

TREE HUGGING

When Sam knotted the rope that bound me to the birch tree, I was able to use the same measures as before to keep the knot and rope tension where I wanted. He left and returned with a number of vessels, some not too clean, which he filled with water and placed on the ground within reach. The tree which I found myself embracing was a slender birch which measured about five inches across the trunk at eye level. 'Not likely to uproot or bite through it,' I thought, 'but maybe there's another way.'

I circled the tree, being careful not to knock over the water containers, until I could watch the trio prepare for the trail. They stripped my own pack, taking anything of obvious value and leaving the mostly empty pack lying on the ground. I watched my thousand-dollar Zeiss binoculars and my Ruana hunting and skinning knife disappear into Pete's pack. The other two threw my tarp tent, Knapp-saw, and the Swedish Optimus cook stove out on the ground along with the other contents without recognizing their utility.

I noticed that the tree I was hugging was out of sight of the main trail— whether by accident or design, I wasn't sure. It was a cinch nobody passing on the main trail could see me, and I doubted my voice would carry that far over the sound of the river.

'Not that I'd know when to yell,' I thought, 'since I can't see the trail from here.'

An hour later, the trio appeared ready for the trail. Their packs were a lot trimmer now than when I had first seen them, so it seemed they had learned a little something from their misfortunes. And they had my matches and can opener, plus the folding spoon and fork unit I always carried in the field. When I got loose (and there wasn't any doubt in my mind that I'd find a way), I'd be in about the same situation, without fire and tools, as they had been.

Pete sent Sam and Eddy on down to the trail, then walked threateningly toward me and my tree. I suspected he might just silently kill me after his crew was out of sight, but he merely stopped, grinned at me, and carefully kicked over each of the water containers that Sam had placed around my open-air prison.

"When you get loose," he said, "if you want your rifle back, just look me up and ask. I'll have it ready for you." He gave a mocking laugh and strode away to join his partners.

HEAVY MONEY

As the trio of bank robbers began their walk north, they still hadn't solved the problem of carrying both the green money bag and their shoulder packs. Sam and Eddy were tired of one or the other being forced off the trail at the narrow spots. Pete, a very large and strong man, could have perched it on a shoulder and managed it along with his trail pack, but he had no intention of doing so. Bosses didn't do work—they made work.

Finally, Eddy threw down his side of the green duffle.

"There's gotta be a better way. Didn't the Indians rig some kinda way to drag stuff behind them?"

"Yeah," said Sam. "The used two poles and slung the load between em. Pulled the load so the back ends of the poles dragged along the ground. We could do that and take turns doing the dragging. Then Pete could get in on the work too."

Pete turned and gave them an icy stare. The junior partners shrugged and took to the brush to find a pair of slender saplings for the drag poles. It did not take long to lash the duffle bag between the poles, but the result was disappointing. The weight of the bag pulled the poles together, the result being something like a loosely slung hammock which dragged one's butt along the ground unless the front was held uncomfortably high. This required re-engineering; other short poles were cut which, when lashed between the main rails, kept them spread and kept the load high.

Pete, propped against his pack in a sunny spot, grew impatient with all the fuss about carrying a 40-pound bag. However, he was smart enough to remain silent lest any of his caustic remarks lead to more talk about the possibility of his helping haul the load.

They recommenced their march, having lost over an hour trying to solve their logistics problem. By early afternoon, they were hardly three miles from their previous camp, the jury-rigged travois proving little better than their former cuss-and-carry technique.

They camped that evening just short of the ford where Ben had crossed several days before. As they prepared for the night, a chorus of wolves tuned up and gave a five- minute concert in the distance. The tents were pitched much closer together this night.

Decisions, Always Decisions

I waited until I thought there was little chance of any of the robbers returning for some forgotten item, or of Pete deciding to come back and eliminate a possible witness.

Pete had tipped over the water containers, but had not bothered to kick them out of reach. I slid my hands down the tree and tucked its bole into my shoulder, pulled all the containers close with my lower legs, and reset them right side up and near enough to reach. I was thankful that Sam had picked a tree small enough that I had a little freedom of reach if I contorted my body and shoulders. Now, if I couldn't get free quickly, I could at least hope for rain and water to drink.

I carefully considered the possible means of escape, not wanting to commit to one and realize later that there was an easier way.

Cutting the tree down was an obvious way, but I had absolutely no cutting implements and no time to train a beaver.

Climbing the tree and trusting my weight to bend it over so I could slip out of the top was a dim possibility. But if I found myself in the tree blocked by a branch I couldn't bend up or break off, I might well be worse off—stuck between limbs and dying with no water in reach and no likelihood of being noticed by any passer-by.

Breaking the nylon rope was impossible.

Cutting it would be nice, if I had something to cut with. Maybe the bent-back lid of one of the water cans? It would be very slow work if it worked at all, and I'd hold that in mind as a last resort.

Of course, rubbing the rope against any rough rock I could find within reach might serve also, if I had a day or two to work.

And fishing the little revolver out of my boot and trying to shoot the rope in two was possible, but was more likely to result in my shooting myself.

My final decision for the first try was what I pretty well knew it was going to be. I had held my hands with wrists placed so the rope would take the long way around when Sam cinched it tight. Now, when I turned my wrists flat-to-flat, about an inch of slack appeared. Nylon rope is slippery—if a knot is not kept tight, any movement of the rope may allow the end to work loose. Pete, or an experienced boater or logger, would never have let me position my wrists as I did for Sam. In fact, they would never have used such thick nylon rope, or tied it with a square knot.

I twisted my wrists inward, palm to palm, and pulled. Not with a steady pull, but with little jiggly movements. I could feel things shifting and loosening. By tucking the tree trunk as far around in my right armpit as possible, I was able to stretch my neck and reach the knot with my teeth. I could never have chewed through that nylon, but it was not hard to nip the soft rope in my teeth and work the end through the knot a little at a time. Once the end pulled through, a steady twisting of my wrists pulled the slick rope through the next loop and the rope slipped free and dropped to the ground.

So did I, in relief and exhaustion. The edges of the can lids would probably have eventually worked, but this was surely the easy way.

My own pack lay on the ground, mostly empty. I searched its pockets for leftover goodies and was gratified to find that my rolled up spare socks were still stuffed down in the corner of the lower compartment. I unrolled them and found the extra ten rounds of 38 Special ammunition that I usually carried there with two spare books of matches. With the four unfired rounds remaining in the revolver, I had 14 potentially lethal shots at my disposal.

I had never been quite sure what armament the bad guys had—I had recognized the nickel-plated Saturday-night-special that Eddy carried as a purely short-ranged weapon—if it worked at all. I had seen, from my view up the barrel, that the cylinder was only partially loaded—two chambers were obviously empty, so there might be three or four live rounds remaining.

Sam had a pocket pistol of some sort, but it was never exposed to my view.

Pete had a large weapon of some sort shoved under his belt, and he now had my rifle and the eight loose cartridges that I had carried in my pockets. He had never checked the chamber in my presence; whether he had later done so and loaded the empty chamber, I couldn't know.

'A lot for my little five-shot Smith to take on,' I thought, 'so best not to start an in-your-face firefight.' But I did replace the light target and small game loads in the cylinder with five jacketed hollow point Plus-P high velocity cartridges from the sock.

I gathered food left behind by Pete and company, who had evidently learned that sometimes more is not better. When I repacked my gear, I looked askance at the number of canned items and flinched at their weight and bulk. I had eaten most of my lightweight rations, and all that I had to choose from now were the trio's abandoned leavings. Luckily, I found the two spare P-38 GI can openers still taped together in the bottom pocket of my pack.

I estimated that my opposition had been on the trail an hour and a half. Having seen their lack of skill and trail wisdom, and knowing that the heavy money bag would slow them, I figured to catch up about the time they set up camp. I eagerly anticipated a night of fun.

About that time, a quiet voice which sounded exactly like Liz began whispering to my inner self.

"Ben, all you have to do now is stroll into town, report those guys to the law, and spend the night in comfort as a guest of the Brandts. Troopers will send a team in with a chopper and have them buttoned up by noon tomorrow"

'But that damn Pete took my Winchester, my knife, and my good binoculars—and he tried to leave me to die of thirst!'

"He also took your pride. That's what's bothering you, isn't it?"

My inner self refused to answer.

I walked down to the main trail, stopped, and scanned the trail and the river. No sign of the robbers. I could turn south and abide by Liz's advice and my own common sense. Or I could turn north and try to catch up with the fugitives, get my stuff back. get my pride back, and maybe get shot for my trouble.

NOISES IN THE NIGHT

Pete and his pals had approached the ford just at that stage of the trek when Sam and Eddy were ready to drop. Pete was in fine fettle, ready for another four miles, but, of course, he carried a much lighter load than his minions. When he suggested another mile or two, he was informed that he was welcome to keep going, but his partners and the money were going to stay right here. Since Pete had no intention of allowing the money bag out of his sight, he allowed as how they had all worked pretty hard and probably earned an early rest.

They pitched their usual sloppy camp, improved only in that they had finally figured out how to rig the tents to provide crude shelter. Pete chose to camp on the near side of the gushing stream where it flowed into the river, mostly because he hadn't yet figured out how to ford it.

"You see all those bear tracks in that soft part of the trail?" asked Eddy. "Must be a bunch of 'em around. Think we oughta set a guard tonight?"

"You guys do what you want. I'm planning to sleep hard and fast— this hiking business has wore me out. If a bear bites you, wake me up and I'll give him a taste of this." He tugged the sawed-off shotgun out of his belt and put it down beside him.

Fishing a couple of cans out of his pack, one of beef stew and one of peaches, he set about using the P-38 can opener on the stew.

"Get a fire going," he ordered between curses, as his big fingers slipped and fumbled with the tiny tool.

Sam walked by on one of his many trips to gather firewood and kindling.

"Say," he remarked over Pete's shoulder, "that little key thing stuck on the bottom of the stew can looks like it might unwind the top of the can."

"I'm doing just fine with the opener," Pete lied, and waited until Sam moved away before detaching the key and quickly stripping the top off the can.

An hour later, after everyone had somehow hacked the top off his can, heated the contents to little more than body temperature, and tossed the empty cans into the forest surrounding the camp, they began to discuss how each planned to spend his share of the bank money. As tired bodies began to overcome vivid imaginations, they crawled into their makeshift sleeping gear and surrendered to fatigue.

Eddy was the first to wake. It seemed to him as though he had barely hit the sack—it couldn't be morning already. He slowly grew conscious of what had awakened him; someone was snoring, the sound reverberating through camp like a tuba. It had to be Sam—Pete seldom snored.

He punched Sam, who immediately came awake.

"What's the trouble?"

The snoring continued. They looked at each other nervously

"Hey, Pete!" they yelled simultaneously

Pete struggled awake, rubbed his eyes, and looked around.

"Who the hellever is snoring, wake him up," Pete grumbled, " I can't sleep with that racket going on."

The snoring continued, the three of them listening and realizing that it was more of a grunting than a snore. And it was occasionally interrupted by a loud huffing noise.

In ten minutes, the fire was burning brightly and the three were sitting with their backs to it, staring into the shadows, weapons in hand. The snorting and huffing gradually quieted, but renewed itself at intervals. During one startling episode during which it came from a different direction, Eddy abruptly stood and emptied his revolver into the night— three shots and a number of hollow clicks.

"Dammit, Eddy, you shot up all your ammo at shadows," complained Pete, "and there ain't no gun stores on this trail. Sam, wait 'till you have a target 'fore you cut loose with yours; you only got seven rounds for that 22, and it'll likely take 'em all to get a bear's attention."

There was no more growling to be heard. Perhaps a random bullet had killed the bear or chased it off, but the memory was sufficient to maintain their nervous attention throughout the night.

Wet Crossing

I rolled out of the sack early, curious to know what effect my night noises might have had on the men camped down by the trail. I'd already figured out their ammo supply from Pete's comments during the night show; the only thing that really worried me was Pete and my 338 Winchester. I'd pretty-well figured out that Pete was the dangerous one. I had no idea how good a shot he might be, but I knew damn well he could outrange me and my little 38 snubbie. I couldn't allow him to get a clear shot at me; any solid hit from the 338 would be a killing hit.

I had no intention of hurting anybody just yet—hoped to just dull them by keeping them awake for another night. Then to get in close and somehow take Pete out, hopefully by disarming him without shots being fired, and to face down the remaining pair. In light of what I had previously seen, I didn't expect much resistance from them.

I could hear distant voices from the direction of their camp, unintelligible but with a clearly angry and impatient overtones. Curious to learn more, I moved downslope to where a gap in the trees revealed the place where they were preparing to ford the feeder stream.

Pete was obviously haranguing his minions to wade the stream—they were just as obviously reluctant until they had some idea of the depth of the water at that particular point. I could see Pete examining the water up and down stream, then selecting the place where the stream was narrowest and the water seemed quietest. A typical greenhorn mistake.

The same volume of water generally flows down a stream at all points; if the stream is narrower at any particular place, then it must be deeper there to let the water pass. A point where the stream is widest is probably the point where it is most shallow and more easily fordable.

Pete had found a spot about a hundred yards upstream where the water seemed quiet, and narrow. He steered his underlings to it and was apparently trying to convince them that "this is the place." What followed was a baptism that would have gladdened the heart of a Baptist preacher. Sam went first, although reluctantly, but he was evidently a passable swimmer. He bounced off the bottom a few times, soaking himself and his gear, but managed to haul himself, his pack, and a length of rope across the relatively slow-flowing water.

Eddy went next, hauling his own pack plus that of Pete. Being less buoyant, he swallowed more water than Sam and spent more time on the bottom. After Sam dragged Eddy up the bank, and they had congratulated each other on still being alive, they turned their attention to their boss, still on the opposite bank. From their huddled consultation, I suspected they were debating the wisdom of leaving things that way and hiking north without him.

Pete was not without a devilish sort of cunning, however—he had arranged the crossing so that, although his pack was on the far side of the stream, the money-filled green bag was still with him. In fact, it was attached to the tail end of the rope which Sam had towed across the stream.

After some minutes of yelling back and forth across the water, Pete embraced the money bag and leaped into the frigid water. The two on the farther bank may have been tempted to let go the rope and watch Pete drift away into the sunset, but they felt a sentimental attachment to the money. They dutifully marched inland, the rope across their shoulders, and hauled their spluttering leader, with money bag, ashore like a surfing walrus.

Their next move, predictably, was to build a roaring fire, strip off their clothing, and try to dry out for the next leg of their journey.

I kicked myself for not being in a position to confront them at this, a most vulnerable moment. Instead, I hunkered down and waited for them to re-energize and continue their trek.

GUESTS

Eddy and Sam sullenly eyed Pete, who busied himself in any way which didn't involve making eye contact with them. He unzipped the money duffle and spread a few dampened bundles of bills out to dry. The waterproof duffle bag had done its job, and only the top layers of bills near the zipper were damp. Pete cheerfully remarked on this bit of luck but received little enthusiasm from his crew who sat silent and shivering in their underwear.

Eddy suddenly cocked his head, listened for a moment, and whispered, "There's somebody up the trail."

The crew froze. Distant voices were heard, rapidly becoming less distant.

A quick glance at their resting area made it plain that there was no hope of cleaning the place up and concealing themselves—the scatter of clothing and gear resembled the residue of a bombed-out laundry.

In desperate haste, the men grabbed still-wet trousers and pulled them on over damp shorts. They were reaching for shirts when a party of four merry hikers stopped short at the sight of the mortified trio.

"Hey," exclaimed the taller of two men, "What kinda party is this anyway? Caught you with your pants down, huh?"

The two women of the party, after a quick glance at the scene, mercifully shifted their gaze to the far bank of the river until Pete's party was more-or-less fully garbed.

The man who had spoken, a lanky person dressed in a new khaki outfit resembling that of a big game hunter in Africa, seemed to be a bit under the weather. He reinforced that impression by producing a flask from his safari jacket and offering all present a taste.

"You've probably had enough of that, Stu," said the second man, smaller by a foot but more heavily built. "We're not to civilization yet."

"What civilization?" was the reply. "I haven't seen anything civilized since I left Seattle. And I need this stuff," he shook the flask, "to keep the bugs away."

His Ivy League accent was enough to stir resentment among Pete's crew, and his disparagement of Alaska added to their ire. The most humble bush rat might criticize Alaska, by himself or with company, but having an outsider do so was apt to lead to the proverbial "unforeseen consequences".

"Shut up, Stuart," said the more slightly built of the two women, but with a finality which indicated that she was accustomed to being obeyed. Stuart immediately did so.

The shorter man put out a hand to Pete.

"I'm Bob Russfield. The loudmouth here is Stuart Whitmore. The ladies, Cynthia," he motioned toward the smaller one, "and", he turned to the taller, "Marge."

No one else offered to shake hands which, considering the appearance of Pete's crew, was understandable.

Pete was confused as to what to do. The money bag was open for all to see and hundred-dollar bills were spread out on the ground around it.

Stu Whitmore, obviously a master of bad timing, picked up a bill and examined it.

"Holy cow! What did you guys do? Rob a bank?"

A SLIGHT COMPLICATION

As I was trying to devise some way of getting across the torrent and approaching Pete's group unseen, a group of four touristy-looking hikers stumbled into their camp from the north. There was some conversation and introductions that I couldn't hear, but when the safari dude picked up a bill and looked closely at it, I could see trouble coming. And I somehow doubted it was the kind of trouble I could overcome with my night games and Indian tactics.

He said something that apparently got Pete's attention; Pete extracted a large handgun of some type from the pile of cast-off clothing and jammed it in the guy's chest. The visitors raised their hands to the heavens while Sam and Eddy searched them, coming up with a huge revolver which had hung on the belt of the tall man.

This was all I needed—the complication of four possible hostages plus the addition of a formidable appearing weapon to the opposing arsenal. My little 38 was getting littler all the time.

I was curious as to how Pete was going to react to his new situation. Would he continue north and force his captives to backtrack along with his crew? If so, what would he do with them when they reached their Cooper Landing destination?

Or would he send them on south, hoping his party would reach the highway and be gone before the tourists could get to Seward and report the encounter?

'No,' I thought to myself, 'that couldn't happen. Pete would never take the risk.'

I shoved the obvious solution out of my mind, but it crowded back in. Pete had to dispose of the intruders directly—either that, or anchor them to trees as he had done me. I didn't really believe that Sam and Eddy would go along with wholesale murder, but I suspected that, when their pack mule functions were no longer needed, Pete had already made terminal plans for them.

I moved down the south bank of the stream, wishing I had crossed earlier, and searched for a place to ford that was screened from the view of the camp. Finding none, I went back upstream and eventually found a bend which combined a wide shallow spot and enough vegetation to block any view from the camp. I went back to my own camp, gathered my gear, and returned to my chosen fording spot.

I crossed using the garbage bag boots that Pete had conveniently left in my pack. Working my way back to the camp was slow and arduous, there being less brush and trees to cover my movements. I finally admitted that I could never get as close as I needed by the feeder stream route, so looped out and approached from the north, as had the tourist group. Using the trail gave me the advantage of silence, and of quick movement if I had to flee.

I was able to get within 20 yards of the group and could easily hear any conversation that went on. At this point, however, there was silence. A small gap in the foliage allowed a very narrow view of the camp, but by moving carefully from side to side, I was able to see about half of the group. Pete was pensively staring into space, a sawed-off double-barreled shotgun in his right hand, a large Smith & Wesson revolver in his left. The two women stood across the fire from him, the smaller with crossed arms and smoldering anger in her eyes. The other, blonde, and busty, fearfully nursing a swelling lip.

Pete broke his stare and looked at the women.

"You ladies," he said the word with contempt, "need to remember who's holding the guns. Next bitch that slaps anybody's gonna get a gun barrel across her face. And you guys," he turned to the men, "don't wanna be heroes. Any bodies get left out here, the bears clean 'em up and nobody ever knows."

He turned to a spot I couldn't see. "Sam, you and Eddy get this place cleaned up. We'll finish drying out and camp here for the night. Set up the tents and have these folks set up theirs."

A Conscience?

Pete had gone rigid at Whitmore's casual remark; Eddy could sense a violent reaction on the way, and did his best to derail it.

"That's stage money. We're part of a movie-making crew. Filming a flick about a big train holdup and the fake cash got wet crossing the creek. The others went on ahead while we stayed back to dry out the money and ourselves."

Stu bent down and picked up a bundle of hundred-dollar bills still in the bank wrapper. He riffed through them.

"Consecutive numbers—sure look real to me."

"That's enough, dammit," said Pete, extracting the sawed-off shotgun from a pile of damp clothing near the fire, 'Suppose you put my money down and stick your hands straight up. All of you! Sam, search their gear."

Pete wasn't sure just what to do with the situation in which he found himself. He was realizing that just keeping his mouth shut and letting Eddy carry the ball would probably have let them continue north with only a little suspicion and puzzlement from the newcomers.

When that dude in khaki started playing with the money, Pete reacted without thought—as usual. Now he had to evaluate the choices left to him. Objective evaluation was not one of Pete's strong suites; sometimes it even made his head hurt.

He couldn't just let them go on to Seward after pulling a gun on them. Taking them north to Cooper Landing was impractical.

He thought about forcing the strangers into the stream one at a time and watching them drown. That might be considered a wilderness accident by the authorities, though it might seem odd that individuals of the party would keep jumping into the rushing torrent after seeing others drown.

Probably better to just march 'em up a canyon somewhere and make 'em disappear. Sam might stand for that, particularly if he didn't have to watch and could later say he didn't know for sure what happened. Sam was pliable.

Eddy was another story, though. He wasn't a very impressive guy, but he had a tough core. If Pete decided to shoot the tourists, he'd probably have to kill Eddy too. Of course, in the back of his mind he'd already considered making both Sam and Eddy disappear when they reached the end of this trail. Just how would depend on the circumstances he was given to work with.

He was jerked back to reality by the smaller woman, the one they called Cindy.

"Hey, you with all the guns. I need to take Marge down to the stream and put some cold water on that bruise you gave her."

"Well, do it! Sam, you go with 'em. Shoot 'em if they decide to run. And, bitch, if she hadn't slapped me, I wouldn't have had to hit her. A lot of fuss over the friendly squeeze of a boob!"

Cynthia gave him a look that would wilt poison ivy and led off to the feeder stream, Sam falling in behind with his 22-automatic in hand.

Eddy began straightening up camp as he was told. He ordered the two men to pitch their tents, having them empty their packs first to insure there were no other weapons at hand. The Smith 44 Magnum that had hung on Whitmore's hip was apparently the only weapon the group possessed. There was a bottle of whisky in Whitmore's pack, and the flask he had been sipping out of. Eddy hid them in a pile of clothing, afraid of what booze might do to Pete's disposition if he got into it.

While they worked, Eddy gave some thought to the problems confronting the trio. He knew that keeping their visitors captive was impractical, and would soon lead to complications he really didn't want to deal with. Pete had already screwed things up beyond the point of a graceful solution. If the robbers were captured, which Eddy now considered more likely than not, the robbery charges would be dwarfed by possible charges of rape and murder. Pete was capable of either during his act-first-and-think-later episodes. Eddy didn't believe Pete actually had any conscience or sense of right or wrong—right was what he wanted, wrong was anything that prevented him from getting it.

Eddy was now effectually disarmed, having fired all his ammunition at the growling shadows during their sleepless night. If he wanted to block Pete's more murderous impulses, he needed to find something to overcome the arsenal hanging from Pete's belt. Or, he could just run. Desert the group and repudiate its actions; make a deal with the law and testify against them.

But, if he ran, Pete would have his way, people would be hurt or killed—maybe him, if Pete caught him.

Somewhere deep inside, Eddy was finding a conscience, a sense of responsibility for others. The feeling was disturbing.

JUST DO IT

I watched the trio walk down to the water's edge, Sam lagging a little and keeping close watch on the women. It seemed like an opportunity to rescue them and take out one of the opposition, to be a hero for the moment. But I put myself in Pete's shoes.

On hearing a shot and finding the women gone, he and Eddy would have to give chase. They couldn't leave the men unguarded, and the simplest solution in Pete's mind would probably be to shoot them, then run down the women. And once Pete pulled the trigger on anyone, that would set the pattern for his future actions.

I could survive, and likely take Pete out eventually, but how many of the captives would pay with their lives? Damn, it's not easy being a hero!

My mental debate must have taken longer than I thought. Before I could decide on a course of action, the ladies stood and started back toward the campfire, Marge holding a wet bandanna to her cheek. Sam dutifully followed along, clutching his pistol and looking around as though he expected a bear attack at any second.

I debated the wisdom of emitting a growl or two from my nest in the brush, but knew the risk of being hit by a random 22 bullet overweighed the fun I'd have watching Sam bolt toward the camp.

While the attention of the camp was directed toward the returning trio, I changed locations and found a spot that afforded a view of the entire camp. I was near enough to score with the 38 snubbie if a shot became necessary, and could hear most of what was said in the camp. All seven were now gathered near the fire and conversation was pretty-well stalled. Pete stole occasional glances at Marge, mostly concentrated on her chest. Sam and Eddy seemed buried in their own thoughts. The women stared into the fire, working hard at being inconspicuous. The two male captives sat shamefaced on their packs, humiliated by their inability to protect the women in their care.

I did a mental inventory of the arms that I would have to face if I chose to step in now. Eddy was empty. Sam still had the 22-pocket pistol, a Beretta from the looks of it. Pete had a sawed-off shotgun, the 44 Magnum revolver, and my Winchester 338 rifle.

The questions in my mind: if I stepped into the open and shot Pete between the eyes, would Sam have the presence of mind to pepper me from behind with the 22? Or would the captives have the presence of mind to jump Sam first? What was Eddy likely to do when the crap hit the fan?

And would Pete collapse like a punctured balloon, or would my shot be off, and would Pete blow me in half with the sawed-off before I could get in a second bullet?

The weak point in my plan was that its failure, for any reason, was as likely to cost the lives of the captives as to cost my own. Was it right to bet other people's lives without their having a say in the matter?

I was beginning to wish that I had obeyed the impulse to turn south on the trail after freeing myself from Sam's ropes. If I had done so, I'd be putting down a martini in Seward right now, and State Trooper choppers would shortly be scooping up the bank robbers and congratulating the freed captives.

I could almost hear Liz grumping, "I told you so."

'Dammit, just do it!' I told myself, 'If you don't, these guys will probably die, and the women will be put through hell—and likely die.'

I pulled my thoughts together, checked the cylinder of the 38-revolver for loads, and silently cocked it. I grasped the walnut grips, snuggled my left hand under my right in a tight two-handed hold, and stood up.

WHEN YOU GOTTA GO

Pete was nervous. His plan for the bank robbery had been carefully thought out, and it should have worked fine. None of the complications which had occurred were his fault—who knew that the bank had put in a sprinkler pipe right where he had fired his gun? And the campground in town where he had wanted the truck fire to start—how could he have known it would be closed? He rubbed his left forearm, the reddened hairless one, which still stung from the heat of the truck fire flare up.

And the matter of the blown-up food cans. How was anybody supposed to have known that could happen when you tried to heat them? And not carrying a can opener when you had to eat from cans? Sam or Eddy should have thought of that. And if the tents didn't work right, whose fault was that? And when the Bic lighter ran dry, why were there no spares?

His idea, his plan, had resulted in a really rich haul from the bank vault; he was proud of that, and his crew should have taken care of those small details that had plagued them on the trail. Hell, he was the boss, and bosses should be able to expect their people to take care of routine stuff.

He sat, Ben's rifle across his knees and the sawed-off jammed in his waistband, the 44 Mag in its holster hanging from his belt. The only other gun in camp was the 22-pistol that Sam carried, so Pete felt reasonably secure. Maybe he should lend the 44 to Eddy, but, somehow, the more guns he controlled, the safer he felt. In fact, he'd feel better yet if Sam was unarmed too.

He looked over at Marge again.

'Now, that's what I call a healthy pair,' he said to himself. 'No falsies there,' recalling the squeeze that had earned him the slap.

'Before I'm done, she'll regret that slap. Or maybe she'll fall in love. I gotta be more of a man than whichever wimp she's with.'

He transferred his gaze to the pair of whipped dogs across the fire, staring into the dirt.

'Upper-crust bastards,' he thought. 'Both together wouldn't make a pimple on a real man's ass. Uppity and snotty in towns, where their money makes 'em big wheels, but good for nothing out here where you need brains and muscle. Wonder if I'll get like that when I hit town with that big bag of money.'

He snickered to himself. 'Damn right I will. And I'll stick it to everybody every chance I get.'

His daydreams were interrupted when the shorter of the two male captives, Bob Russfield, raised his hand like a kid in school.

"I gotta go," he said.

"Well, go. Sam, you go with him—make sure he comes back."

Sam appeared discomforted by the idea of going out to watch another man pee, but said nothing. He gestured Russfield toward the woods and followed reluctantly.

Eddy wondered how Pete would handle it when one of the women had to go. He had no wish to embarrass, or to be embarrassed, by having to guard a lady with her pants down. But he definitely didn't like the idea of Pete being the sole escort. He hoped it would be Sam, who had the only other gun.

He could see by fleeting expressions on the women's faces that they were turning the same question over in their minds.

YOU GOTTA GO

I was a split second from leaping into the camp ala Tarzan, trying to kill Pete and maybe Sam, when Bob raised his hand. I quickly hunkered down again, praying nobody had noticed my sudden movement in the brush. Once the pair left the camp, my plan was useless. Killing Pete now would still leave an armed opponent in the woods, ready to pop me at the first opportunity.

All the skill in the world couldn't reliably protect against a shot in the back from an unseen enemy. I had seen that scenario played out too often in the past to invite it now. And if I were killed, the chances of the captives surviving were near zero.

I was contemplating other plans of action when I heard a shot from the woods where Sam and Bob had disappeared a few moments ago. The camp was frozen for a few seconds, until Pete unholstered the 44 Magnum and tossed it to Eddy.

"Get out there and see what happened," he ordered, "and don't lose that gun."

Eddy deftly caught the big handgun and ran out of the camp in the direction of the shot. I listened for more shots, especially for the boom of the big "Dirty Harry Special", a name bestowed after Clint Eastwood had made the 44-Magnum revolver famous in his movie, "Dirty Harry".

There was silence from the woods, then voices, and all three men emerged from the bush and joined the tense group by the fire.

Sam had a sheepish expression as he explained to Pete.

"I had to take a leak too, and he jumped me and tried to get the gun while I was busy. I didn't have the safety on, and it went off—clipped his leg a little, I think."

Eddy chimed in. "When I got there, they were busy apologizing to each other. I looked at Bob's leg. Just a cut and some powder burns right above the ankle. He'll be OK."

"Whatta you trying to do?" asked Pete, looking at Russfield. "Be a damn hero and rescue the women from the big bad bank robbers? I oughtta put you down right now.

"And you, Sam, can't even watch a guy taking a leak without screwing up! You're lucky I didn't come in there and shoot you both. Next time any of you four try any fancy moves on us, we'll bury the whole bunch and not have to worry about you anymore."

He reached for the 44 in Eddy's hand.

"Maybe I'd better keep this, Pete, unless you wanna pull my guard shift tonight. Can't guard these people with nothing but a big rock in each hand."

Pete hesitated. I could see he was nervous about any of the others being armed, and I had a good idea why.

"OK, but be careful how you handle it. Damn 44 will shoot through a couple of people plus a pine tree—we don't need any accidental slugs flying around here."

"Speaking of," said Eddy, "did you know one of the hammers on that hand cannon stuck in your belt is still cocked? It goes off, you'll likely lose something important."

Pete looked down with alarm, and saw that Eddy was correct. He carefully withdrew the sawed-off and eased the left hammer down to the safe position. Everyone tried to hide their grins as he shoved the gun back into his waistband.

From my hiding place, I watched with disappointment. I had noticed the cocked hammer earlier, and was hoping Eddy's prediction would come to pass, giving me a grand opportunity to get into the game with much less risk.

To cover his embarrassment, Pete grinned, leered at the women.

"Thanks, Eddy. Who knows, I just might need that old thing shortly."

THREE'S A CROWD

The day had been cloudy, and dusk fell early. The emotions and uncertainties of the day had drained everyone, and the relief of sleep was anticipated. After the contents of the four newly-arrived backpacks had been gone through, and the choicest food items claimed by their captors, the newcomers went through the leavings and found enough to satisfy their own hunger.

Pete rolled up in the warmest appearing sleeping bag without designating any guard shifts. Eddy and Sam looked at each other questioningly.

"Oh, hell," said Eddy, "I'll take first shift." He looked at his watch. "Wake you at midnight."

Sam looked relieved and searched out his own bedding, while Eddy propped himself up near the fire, 44 Magnum in his lap. The captives found sleeping gear and started to do the same.

"Hey, Eddy," called Marge, from the opposite side of the fire, "I have to go to the bushes before I turn in."

"Me too. I'll go with you," said Cindy quickly, thinking that two women might be less apt to be molested than one.

"Sam, keep an eye on the guys—I'll go with 'em." said Eddy.

"Just hold it," came a growl from Pete's direction. "I'll go with 'em."

"I'll take care of it , Pete," said Eddy quickly. "I'm already up."

"The hell you will. Can't trust you around helpless women."

Eddy, holding the 44 loosely in his right hand, drew himself up to his full five and a half feet. "Pete, I'LL DO IT!"

His tone of voice was one that Pete had not heard during their entire acquaintance, and it was sheathed in iron. Pete looked at him, and at the big revolver, hanging in a non-threatening but ready position.

"OK; just trying to let you guys have a little more sleep, since you're pulling night guard." He burrowed back down into sleeping bag.

Eddy gave him no time to change his mind. He waved the ladies toward the woods, handing each a wad of toilet paper as they passed, and fell in behind them.

The women wandered about a bit, apparently looking for just the right place, like fussy spaniels. When they finally found a spot to their liking, they stopped and looked at him; he raised his hands and smiled apologetically.

"Ladies, you can see why I can't turn my back on you. But I'll keep my eyes away and maybe you can kinda shield one another."

This brought a few seconds of rolling eyeballs and a "Yeah, sure." expression, but Eddy fastened his gaze on a nearby stump and managed to keep it there while the women accomplished their mission. When all was done, and he had shepherded them back to the campfire, Marge laid a hand on his arm and whispered a barely audible "Thank you for being such a gentleman."

Pete roused long enough to give them a suspicious look, and reburied himself in his bedding. The male captives give the girls and Eddy a questioning look, then searched out their own sleeping gear and retired.

Eddy hunkered back against a handy tree and settled into his role as sentry. He wondered at all the curious and questioning looks they had just received. What were these people expecting? It wasn't as though the three had been cavorting around in the woods naked. Taking a pee or a dump in the woods wasn't exactly the kind of strip show that would get anybody all excited.

And he felt oddly touched by Marge's thanks—he could still feel the warmth of her hand on his arm. He didn't recall ever being referred to in the past as a gentleman, and wouldn't have called himself such, but it felt comforting coming from Marge.

He wasn't even sure what defined a gentleman—maybe just making the effort to be decent to people? More than just proper speech and expensive clothing, he was sure. He had known many men with those characteristics, and he had known for sure that they were no gentlemen. He was sure that the key lay in treating people right, but was not sure what else might come into it. Education, maybe?

He spent most of his shift on guard thinking about the factors that might go in to being a "lady" or a "gentleman".

WAITING

Watching the small dramas unfolding in Pete's camp had been interesting, and the tension of my trying to find just the right time to break in on them was like pre-battle stress during the war—waiting was sometimes more wearing on the nerves than the action itself. I had had enough for one night. I found a spot a quarter-mile up the slope to camp for the night. A cold camp, since I didn't dare start a fire, but a Baby Ruth bar and a night's sleep would be enough for now.

In the morning, I distracted myself from the lack of a cup of hot coffee by considering what I should try now, and how to try it. With guns in the hands of three separate individuals, charging into the camp like an angry grizzly didn't seem all that smart. When I made my move, I didn't want the odds to be even. This wasn't a Roy Rogers movie where the hero shoots the gun out of the villain's hands and never, ever shoots anybody in the back—if I had to shoot, I intended to shoot whoever I had to in any place I could shoot him, and under any conditions.

These people had seemed like the three stooges when I first met them; Pete's willingness to leave me to die painted him a different color in my mind, and the fact that the other two were going along with Pete's program did no credit to them.

I thought back to my first night on the trail, when I lay in my sleeping bag and conducting a mental philosophical debate on justifications for killing. Philosophy and theory were wonderful mental and moral exercises, but were awfully hard to apply in life-or-death situations—especially if the lives involved were not yours.

I recalled a memorable question from an old movie in which the action took place during the Civil War, a war in which several of my ancestors were involved.

"Is it right to kill one man to free another?"

The movie had left the question largely unanswered, although thousands of Yankees had seemed to think the answer was yes. Just as thousands of rebels thought killing necessary if your homeland was invaded. Maybe there was no right answer; a man did what he had to at the time, and he lived with the consequences.

I made up my mind to hover close, mentally prepared to jump in and try to take out everyone who was armed when the time seemed right. Hell, I couldn't prepare and rehearse for every eventuality–all that was left was to be alert and let my gut trigger my actions when the opportunity came.

I managed to get close to Pete's camp while they were stumbling through breakfast. The smell of coffee, obviously provided by the newcomers, was almost enough to convince me I should attack before it got cold, but I managed to resist and to just hang around and hope to overhear Pete's plans for the day.

Pete remained mostly silent, apparently lost in thought; idle chatter from the captives filled the time, chatter with a forced cheerfulness that was an obvious cover for deep concern.

"Hey," said Cindy to Bob, "I'll bet you never figured to play cops and robbers in the boonies when you picked us up in The Double Muskie last week."

"When we picked YOU up? You mean when you picked us up. You girls were trolling for drinks and dinner, and you know it!"

"Yeah, and what were you two trolling for?"

Stu jumped into the conversation.

"I was trolling to have my dream vacation; a long hike in the wilderness of Alaska with something soft and warm in my sack every night."

Marge chimed in, "Well, you could have just shacked up in a motel in Anchorage if that's all you were looking for. I was hoping to meet a guy I liked, and maybe get to know better. You sure don't measure up, Bub."

Cynthia remained silent, though her expression expressed disgust at the entire conversation.

I listened, somewhat puzzled. These people had gotten together, apparently, with expectations varying from a quickie in the woods to hopes of true love. From their present conversation, it seemed that a couple of days on the trail had very effectively ripped away both their lustful and their romantic illusions—they had gotten to know each other much too well.

Bob Russfield finally spoke up, addressing himself to Cynthia.

"Sorry, Cindy. We seem like a right pitiful bunch right now, don't we? I'll admit I was thinking more of a good time than anything else. And it could have been a good time for both of us. Then the fickle finger of Fate threw us in with these. . . outlaws, I'd guess you'd call 'em."

Pete suddenly stood.

PETE'S SOLUTION

Pete was in a quandary—he didn't really want to kill any of the four prisoners, not out of mercy, but because it would add murder to the charges if they were ever caught. And because he lusted after the buxom Marge, who might be less than enthusiastic knowing he had murdered her companions.

Not that he expected her to be cooperative at first, but he was sure his manliness would bring her around after the first time or two.

He needed to find a way to take out the other three without Marge knowing what had happened. It might be manageable only if he could be sure of the obedience of his two subordinates.

The chatter of his unwilling guests was starting to get on his nerves, distracting him from the unaccustomed task of thinking and planning. He stood.

"Shuddup! I'm trying to think of what to do with you damn tourists. Keep pissing me off and I'll take the easy way out."

He walked over to the pile of backpacks and camp gear, rummaging through Stu's gear until he found the flask that Eddy thought he had hidden. He resumed his former place, took three gulps of the not-too-bad whisky, and jump-started his brain again.

The camp was silent for the next half-hour, watching fearfully as Pete cogitated, alternating between swigs of whisky and expressions of deep thought. He finally arose, emptied the flask of its last few drops, and flung it into the brush.

"OK people, here's what we're gonna do. You three," he pointed to the two men and Cindy, "are gonna go to the camp we just left, back toward Seward. You'll take all your gear, and you'll camp there until you run outta food. Then you can go on into Seward—it's only a day's hike.

This one", he pointed to Marge, "will stay with us as a hostage. We'll go on north to Cooper Landing taking her with us."

He stared around at the group.

"Do you understand what I'm getting at? You rat on us, Marge will probably drown if she doesn't get hit by a stray bullet or fall off a cliff. When you hear on the news that she's been released in Cooper or wherever, you can squawk all you want. Maybe write a book or sell your story to the press; I don't give a damn."

Pete's audience listened with fascination—his plan would give most of the captive's freedom from their constant dread regarding their future. It gave no such relief to Marge, who had a good idea of Pete's plans regarding her future.

Bob spoke up almost immediately.

"Why don't you take me instead of Marge. She's bad on the trail— she'll slow you down. You'll make better time with me as hostage."

Pete just looked at him with contempt, shook his head and walked away. Stuart looked relieved; Cindy was horrified and showed it.

Sam was definitely relieved. It made sense to him, and was a lot less messy than Sam had anticipated. Plus, he had no hard decisions to make that might keep him awake nights.

Eddy knew better. Once the captives were out of Pete's control, there was no way he would trust them not to spread the word. Pete himself wouldn't hesitate to betray anyone if the price were right, so he couldn't imagine trusting others not to do the same. And if the other three were to be killed, there was no barrier to Pete's killing anyone else who might be a witness to his actions. And Marge was sure to be killed after Pete was through with her, unless she turned willingly to him. Eddy was somehow sure that would never happen, though he couldn't tell you why.

Eddy's own skin was precious enough to him that he wasn't about to do anything precipitous unless he had to. He needed to know Pete's intentions for sure before considering any plan to thwart him, but he couldn't just stand by and wait for the first shot to be fired.

"OK, you three," said Pete, "Pack your goods. I'll take you to your new camping spot and leave you. Eddy, you and Sam stay with that Marge woman until I get back. And keep your hands off her! Tomorrow morning, we'll head north. Everybody got it?"

Eddy got it for sure. Pete would normally have sent Sam or himself— probably both—back town the trail with the men and Cindy. He himself would remain in camp, lazing around and keeping an eye on the money, and more especially on Marge. If he was going to escort the three captives himself, then hike back here, it was for a reason. And the reason had to be that there was something to be done that he didn't trust Sam or Eddy to do—or that he didn't want them to know about.

And the final proof, to Eddy, was that Pete was willing to leave the bank loot behind while he was gone. Pete had never let the green bag out of his sight and control since the heist.

Pete was going to dispose of the three captives where nobody would see or know.

Eddy silently pondered his dilemma. He wanted his share of the bank money—after all, he had worked for it. He did not want to be caught and pull jail time. But he couldn't live with the knowledge that three innocent people were about to die so all his wants could be met. He had to do something, and quickly.

'Screw it,' he thought, 'Last week I was broke, but I was doing OK. Coulda got a job if I needed money, coulda found a girl if I needed company, coulda left Pete's bunch and connected with a better partner if I had the gumption.

'Now I got more money than God, but I'm up to my butt in a nasty business that'll never let me sleep good again if I let it happen.'

By the time Eddy had made his decision, Pete and the three captives had crossed the stream and disappeared down river.

JUST YOUR BONES

When I overheard Pete's solution to his logistics problem, I knew damn well that he planned to do away with the captive men and Cindy. And probably me if he found me still wrapped around the birch sapling.

Would my best course be to follow him and his captives along the trail south and hope to find the right time and place to face him? Or take off now and intercept him at the old camp?

'No, Stupid,' I told myself. 'He's lazy. He might decide to save the long walk, stop, take them off on some side trail, and have the job done before I even know about it. I'll have to just stay on his heels the whole time and hope to jump in at the right moment.'

I hurriedly forded the stream again (damn, I was getting tired of crossing that cold torrent) and got into position to fall in behind the group once they started. I watched the group clumsily cross the stream, getting themselves thoroughly wet from the hips down, and start south.

Pete took his time herding the three captives along the trail. I heard him call out several times for them to slow down—I imagine they were upbeat at the thought of imminent separation from their captor, and were walking rather briskly toward their goal. The fact that Pete was not in any hurry told me that he didn't plan to travel too far on this mission. I was glad I had chosen to tag along so closely.

After about an hour on the trail, I heard Pete order the party to stop for a break. This was my chance; if Pete flopped down to rest, which he was good at, I should be able to move in behind him and either kill him or hold him at gunpoint and disarm him.

I gave them five minutes to settle down before quietly starting to work my way up to where I could see how they were dispersed. I had taken two steps forward when the brush on my left parted and Pete appeared, jamming the muzzles of the sawed-off shotgun into my neck.

His eyes widened and he appeared as surprised as I.

'You! What the hell are you doing here? How'd you get loose?"

"I did what you suggested—I gnawed through the tree trunk like a beaver."

I should have known not to get flippant with a man like Pete. He removed the muzzles from my neck and jabbed me hard in the pit of the stomach, knocking the breath out of me and putting me on my back.

"Don't be a wise-ass. I asked you a question."

When I could breathe and speak again, I lied to him as sincerely as I could.

"Used the lid from one of the cans you left. Sawed through the rope."

I didn't see any need of telling him the truth—if I ended up with bound wrists again, I might need to reuse the knot trick.

With one hand and shoulder, Pete jerked me off the ground and shoved me up the trail to where the remainder of party waited. They turned toward me in surprised curiosity as he spun me around and threw me to the ground. I made a promise to myself never to get into a one-on-one with this guy—he had the strength of a gorilla, tossing me around with one arm like I was a bundle of rags, still holding the shotgun ready.

"I figured I'd better check the backtrail in case one of my idiots decided to take a hand in the game," said Pete. "Never thought it would be you. Never expected to see your face again." He grinned. "Just your bones, maybe."

BETWEEN YOUR EYES

Pete was cheerfully satisfied at the latest turn of events. The possible survival or escape of the Hunnicutt guy had been a small worry eating away at one corner of his mind. Now the dummy had showed up exactly where Pete needed him—as the fourth target in what was to be a firing squad.

He roused the party with a genial order.

"OK, folks, let's be on our way. We're burning daylight!"

Proud of himself to have remembered the appropriate John Wayne quote, he waved the men to their feet, assisting the woman with a friendly pat on her rear, and herded them south along the trail. After about 20 minutes, he shunted them off the main path and up a faint game trail which seem to lead into a narrow gulch several hundred feet up the mountainside.

"We're gonna rest up there for a while," he said, "maybe take a siesta."

His prisoners appeared puzzled, but were willing to take another rest if the opportunity came. Just past the mouth of the gully the ground flattened somewhat, forming a bowl surrounded by rocky bluffs. He directed his charges to sit around the edges of the open area, backs against the bluff, making sure Hunnicutt was directly in front of him.

"Now, I want you all to take everything out of your pockets and put it on the ground in front of you. Then take your packs and stack them back over there". He pointed to the foot of a rock fissure that ran down one side of the bluff.

As he talked, the unease on the faces of the party turned to alarm. He saw that Hunnicutt showed no expression whatsoever, and knew that the man had guessed what was coming. Pete watched carefully as pockets were emptied and packs moved to the designated location, their owners resuming their seats on the ground around the bowl.

Pete knew he had to first shoot the ones that might cause trouble, depending on the others to plead or cringe in fear while he reloaded or switched weapons—the shotgun only held two rounds, and the rifle had to be manipulated between shots. He decided to take out Hunnicutt first, using the shotgun, then Bob, then use the rifle on that lanky loudmouthed asshole, Stuart Whitmore. The Cindy woman would be last; he might play with her a little first—get something back for all the dirty looks and comments she had thrown at him.

He unslung the Winchester and put it on the ground beside him, handy to be grabbed after the sawed-off had been emptied. Swinging his gaze to Hunnicutt, he smiled broadly while shifting the shotgun from hand to hand suggestively, then slowly bring both hammers to full cock.

"Guess what, Mister Honeybucket? You get to lead the parade."

He waited for a response, or some sign of fear. Hunnicutt was silent, moving only to draw his knees up and wrap his arms about them as though bracing himself for the coming shot.

"If you think your legs are gonna stop a 12-gage slug, you gotta lot to learn, shithead. I'll just put it between your eyes."

As he began to level the shotgun, a flash of movement to his right caught his attention. Taking advantage of Pete's concentration on the stranger, Cindy came to her feet and rifled a fist-sized rock straight into Pete's face. The rock smacked into Pete's jaw with a sound like a dropped ripe melon just as the sawed-off boomed out its heavy, soft lead slug.

From that moment, life became very complicated for Peter Paul Peterson.

FAST BALL

From the moment Pete turned us off the main trail and up toward the small bowl on the side of the mountain, I had known exactly what he planned. The bowl, located at the top of a small gully, was actually a pleasant spot. Sheltered from the wind, with a beautiful view of the river and the valley beyond, and with a small clear snowmelt stream running through it. It would be an ideal campsite, or, if one must die, a pretty spot to die in.

But a better spot for Pete to die in, if I could arrange it. My little 38 revolver was still nestling in its recess in my right boot top, but an opportunity to unobtrusively retrieve it without starting a firefight had never come. The custom-fitted boot pocket had never been designed as a quick-draw rig, just as a convenient way to carry a small gun with a lightweight alloy frame, especially to carry it in places where people weren't supposed to carry guns. But it's a bit hard to stop walking, reach down into your boot, and pull out a gun without drawing some attention.

After Pete had arranged us to his liking, sitting on the ground like ten-pins waiting for the ball, I knew I was out of options. I had to grab the 38 and make my try right now. When Pete singled me out as number one on his "hit" parade, I drew up my knees and draped my arms around them, the fingers of my right hand probing the boot top.

With the sawed-off already levelled at my nose, I never would have made it to the 38 but for the distraction of a gutsy Cindy, rising and pitching her fast ball at Pete's head.

Pete squalled like a branded calf, his broken jaw hanging lopsided on his face. The unaimed slug from his shotgun passed between Cindy and Stu, ricocheting off a nearby boulder and whining down the valley like an angry hornet.

I had the 38 out, snapped two badly aimed shots at Pete, but was puzzled because I could have sworn I heard three. Pete spun around and began running back down out of the bowl and toward the river, stopped for a moment on hearing a voice from below, and throwing a shot toward the voice.

FIREFIGHT

It had taken Eddy a while to bolster his courage, and to do what he knew must be done. He told Sam his plan, and met no resistance from him.

"Pete's gotta be stopped," Sam agreed, "The heist went great, but that was only money. Now he's gonna turn this job into a massacre."

He looked shamefacedly at Eddy. "But I ain't the man to do it."

Marge, who had been listening wide-eyed, approached, and touched Eddy on the arm.

"He's going to kill them." She stated it as a fact, not a question.

Sam averted his eyes and turned away. Eddy reluctantly nodded.

"I'm pretty sure," he said.

"And I know what he has in mind for me," she said, staring into the distance.

"And when he's done, he'll have to kill me too, because I'm a witness to it all."

Eddy and Sam were silent—there was no possible response.

Eddy turned, pulled the heavy revolver from its holster, and checked the loads.

"I'm going after them," he said quietly. "Sam, take her and start north in case I don't come back and Pete does. Hide the money around here somewhere and take what gear and food you two will need."

"Hell, no," Marge erupted, "I'm going with you. I can shoot. Sam, give me that pistol."

Eddy immediately objected, giving half-dozen reasons why she should not. When he turned to leave, she snatched the 22-automatic from Sam's belt and followed him.

"No! You can't go!"

"You can't stop me. I'll just follow along behind. And people could be dying while we stand here yelling at each other."

Eddy gave up; they plunged recklessly across the stream and took up the pursuit.

Eddy set a killing pace, hoping Marge would tire and fall back, be farther from any action that might take place. He was successful; she gradually fell behind as he pushed himself harder.

He soon realized that the pace he set was beyond his usual capacity—the sense of guilt for what might happen was a spur, pushing him beyond his usual limits.

Marge dropped further behind, finally losing sight of Eddy. She slowed, knowing that she would be of no use to anyone if she arrived completely exhausted. She plodded along, pistol in hand, watchful lest she blunder into an encounter which could ruin Eddy's plan.

In truth, Eddy had no plan. He had the big 44 Magnum, but had never fired such an arm and had no idea if he could hit with it unless the target was big and close. Eddy definitely didn't like the idea of getting to within arm's reach of Pete, but if that's what it took . . .

He saw where the group had left the main trail and he cautiously followed uphill until he heard voices, Pete's voice in particular. When in sight of the speaker, he saw that Pete had spread the captives out on the ground before him. He was surprised to see four instead of three, and more surprised to see that the fourth was the Hunnicutt guy from their first camp.

Pete was obviously about to get down to the killing—he cocked the hammers of the sawed-off and leveled it at Hunnicutt's head. Eddy threw up the 44 and fired, the recoil throwing him off balance. At the same time, he heard a flurry of shots from above and saw Pete turn and run down the slope toward him. Fearing he was about to be attacked, Eddy brought the 44 to bear on Pete and yelled at him to drop the shotgun. Pete swung it around and fired once. There was an odd-sounding explosion, Pete yelled, dropped the sawed-off, and bolted down the slope.

THE FINAL SHOT

The old shotgun, having valiantly held together under the stress of two modern high-pressure smokeless hunting loads, gave up. The left barrel split, curling back like a peeled banana, dispersing hot powder gasses and bits of antique iron like a mini-hand grenade.

The fragments of James Purdey's masterpiece saturated the area, and Pete's size made him a large target. His right hand, the one which had pulled the trigger, was relatively unscathed; his left, which had clutched the wood forearm, was unlikely to clutch much of anything else for a while. His front, from belly to kneecap, including his most tender appendages, were peppered with bits of jagged steel and aged walnut. Some of the bits had found his already mangled face, and he could no longer see out of his aiming eye.

THE HUNT

I checked to see if anyone was hit, scooped up my rifle, ran to the lip of the bowl hoping to get a clear shot at Pete. A glance revealed Eddy, standing transfixed, 44 in hand, and Pete stumbling down the hill toward the main trail below. Eddy came to life and fired five deliberate shots at the running man, but Pete never faltered, and disappeared into the brush along the main trail.

I joined Eddy and we plunged down the mountain in pursuit of Pete. As we ran, Eddy gave me a quick account of how he had come to join us. He wasn't that coherent, still breathless from his haste on the trail, and from the desperate climb up to Pete's chosen killing ground. When we struck the main trail, I stopped.

"Do you reckon he'll head back to Seward for medical help, or. . .?"

"He'll head back to the money," said Eddy. "No doubt in my mind. When he has his hands on the green bag, then he might think about getting himself doctored, but who knows?"

"His jaw is broken," I said. "He won't be able to eat until he gets it adjusted and wired up. Just soup, maybe. He's not armed now that he dropped the shotgun, but he's strong and mean enough to force Marge and Sam to help him any way they can. One of my shots might have hit him, but I doubt it. I was scared shitless and shooting wild."

"Marge!" Eddy exclaimed. "She was following me on the trail—couldn't keep up. If she runs into Pete, he'd hold her hostage if he could get his hands on her."

"Oh, damn!" I exclaimed. "That's all we need. Now, if we find that he's holding her, we'll have to kill him quick before he can. . ."

Eddy was already moving north as I spoke, and at a rate that sorely tried my own. As he went, he threw back over his shoulder, "She's got Sam's 22-pistol—might be able to stop him if she has the nerve to use it."

We spotted traces of blood as we hurried down the trail, confirming, if nothing else, that we were going in the right direction. The blood consisted of only minor drops and splatters, so I knew I hadn't hit him with either of my panicky shots from the 38.

'Helluva gunfighter you are,' I thought, 'missing a bull-sized man twice at a range of six feet! Cindy did more damage with her rock than you, a trained soldier and a crack marksman, could do with your precision revolver.'

I stopped Eddy long enough to reload the 38 and hand it to him.

"Here. It's loaded with five. I suggest you get up close, cock it for each shot and aim—I've seen you shoot."

A SHOT IN THE BUTT

Pete was in pain. His face was smashed, two people had shot at him, and his baby, his specially-crafted hand-cannon, had blown up in his hand. Somebody was gonna pay, and pay big!

He'd figured out that he wasn't going to die—all the wounds seemed shallow and weren't bleeding much, and none of the bullets that had been flying around had hit him, but the busted jaw was excruciating and trying to talk or move it made it worse. He still couldn't see out of his right eye, and probing it had convinced him that a piece of wood or steel was buried in the eyeball.

When he had been on the trail long enough to get his wind back, he stopped and listened for sounds of pursuit. He heard scuffling footsteps approaching, but from an unexpected direction. He spun around in time to see Marge appear over a low rise in the trail. She was looking down at footprints as she walked and didn't notice the waiting man until nearly withing reach. When she looked up, she saw Pete's bloody face, lopsided and attempting a painful grimace that might have been a triumphant grin, one eye a bloody pulp.

Marge's heart nearly stopped when he reached out to grasp her—she flung herself into the heavy brush beside the trail, falling but pulling herself upright and retreating from the horrible apparition that had been Pete. He crashed into the brush behind her, bulling his way through and holding up when she stopped, pinned against the river behind.

Pete tried to speak, but the effort was too painful, ending in an animal-like growl.

"Where are the others?" Marge asked, her voice cracking, "Did you kill them? Did you kill Eddy?"

Pete stood silent for a few moments, then, never one to miss the chance to intimidate, slowly nodded his head with another attempt at grin.

His attempt turned to an expression of abject fear when Marge plucked Sam's 22 automatic from a side pocket, deliberately disengaged the safety, and aimed it at him.

Pete's reflexes were good, having been recently sharpened by the large adrenalin dump back at the intended kill site. He turned and dived into the brush just as Marge fired the first shot, scrambled back to the trail, and bolted north toward the stream camp. Pete was a fast and difficult target, having been greatly accelerated by her initial bullet burying itself in his right buttock. Marge rushed back to the trail with every intention of embedding the remaining slugs in the same general area, but Pete had disappeared over the rise in the trail. When she topped the rise looking for him, he was not to be seen.

Despondent at the thought of her friends lying dead somewhere along the trail, and especially Eddy, for whom she had developed a fondness which she found hard to describe, Marge stood alone in the trail, too numb to think.

The clump-clump of trotting boots brought her back to the world; she turned, raising the pistol again against who-knew-what, and was shocked to see Eddy and a stranger running toward her.

"Marge! You OK? We heard a shot," Eddy asked, extending his arms toward her. Without a thought, Marge sought the arms, pressing her head against his chest.

"Eddy! He told me he had killed you. Killed you all. But you're alright?"

"Good as gold, thanks to Cindy. But what happened here?"

Marge explained the encounter, adding that she had shot at Pete when he claimed to have killed everyone.

"What did Cindy do," she asked. The stranger explained about the life-saving rock.

"Oh," she said, "Cindy told me she used to pitch for a women's baseball team down in Florida."

"Well, she's got a helluva fast ball," he said.

"When you shot at Pete, did you hit him?".

"I hit him once in the ass," she said, "but it didn't slow him down. I think it speeded him up." She handed Eddy the pistol. He handed it back after checking the magazine.

"Still six bullets left—keep it. You may need it again if Pete's still alive.

Marge, this is Ben Hunnicutt. Pete tied him up and left him to die. But he didn't."

After that short introduction, the trio started north, hoping Pete hadn't arrived already and killed Sam.

THE CACHE

Sam Duncan was leaning against the bole of a large spruce tree worrying. He had been pacing back and forth along the river bank worrying, but it occurred to him that he could worry just as well while sitting, and it was less strenuous.

What should he do if Pete showed up at the camp? He was now unarmed, having loaned his pistol to Marge, and the last sight he had of Pete, the sawed-off shotgun and Hunnicutt's rifle were in his hands. Since Marge was gone, he had no one to guard except himself—maybe he should just go and hide in the woods and wait to see who returned from that deadly expedition. After all, there was some slight chance that Eddy might have successfully thwarted Pete's plan, not that Sam would have bet a nickel on it.

On the other hand, he was in a position to zip up the money bag and head north, leaving the others to work things out however they chose. That choice was quickly rejected; his experience on the trail had taught him that he might be able to haul the money to civilization, or to carry enough food and shelter to complete the journey, but never both.

A new idea dawned; he could hide the money somewhere nearby, walk out to civilization later, and return to collect it at some future date of his own choosing. But if this were to be done, it must be done quickly—Eddy and Marge, or Pete, could return at any time. Being caught in the act would take more explanation than he was prepared to invent.

Before he could think about the scheme, or talk himself out of it, Sam closed the green bag, heaved it onto a shoulder, and carried it north along the trail. After fifteen minutes or so, he found a game track leading up the slope to his right and into a rocky draw. He followed it upward until he was out of breath, stopped, and looked about him. The draw cut through a small hillock which was unusually flat on top, a feature making it easy to recall and relocate.

The cut was barren of vegetation and seemed a natural water drain, the side banks being dry and bare. Sam noted a spot high on the right bank where some animal had once made or started a den. The hollowed-out space seemed about the right size to tuck the green duffle into. He hauled himself and the bag up to the hollow, scooped out the loose dirt with his hands, and stuffed the bag up inside. He piled loose rocks and gravel against it for concealment, descended to the bottom, and checked out his work.

A quick survey assured him that the bag was well hidden from anyone who didn't know exactly where to look. Feeling self-satisfied with both his idea and its execution, he briskly walked back to camp to gather his gear for the trek out to civilization. He felt like a new man—never again could he be accused of being a no-account drifter, lacking ambition and good only at being a gofer for better men.

CHASE

Pete made his way up the trail at a stumbling trot. The 22-caliber bullet in his butt produced its share of pain, but not that much more than the multitude of other wounds which infested his body. Apparently, it had hit nothing important, and Pete's rear contained enough blubber to absorb a few more if necessary.

'Damn that woman,' he thought. 'She was the only good thing that happened once we started this blasted hike. Not much chance of her warming up to me after today. Why did I have to tell her I killed everybody?

'Now, I gotta gear up, get Sam to grab the money bag, and take off north before that bunch behind gets its shit together and tries to stop me. Need a doc to fix my jaw and plug the rest of the holes, and I'll be OK.'

He crossed the feeder stream with the skill of practice, aided by the fact that the mid-day water level was considerably less than it had been during the previous three days, and that he had no pack.

"Sam!" he attempted to roar as he entered the camp, but the pain in his jaw abbreviated it to an incoherent "Saghhh!" He cupped his hands under his jaw, bracing it somewhat into its normal position, and tried again with much better success, but with no reply.

Sam was not there. Neither was Marge—but he knew that already, didn't she just put a bullet in his ass? But neither was the money duffle, nor Sam's pack. As understanding hit him, Pete let loose a powerful "Goddammit" which might have been more effective had it not come out transformed into a roar of pain and frustration. The bastard had taken the bank loot and headed north to Cooper Landing and civilization. And being alone, he could probably slip through without being caught.

Pete slowly and carefully sat down on the cool earth and pondered the situation. His head began to hurt, along with everything else.

Sam would be unarmed. It was Sam's pistol that Marge had treacherously turned on him. Eddy had the 44. Hunnicutt probably had the rifle back by now. And Pete's own treasure, the sawed-off shotgun, had let him down in his hour of need. So, if he caught Sam, it would just be Sam and Pete. And that would be no contest!

If he took the time to get his gear together, assemble a pack, and set off after Sam, Sam would have yet another hour's lead on him, and Pete wasn't feeling too spry. He'd better just take off now and run Sam down before he got too far ahead. Once he caught Sam, he'd finish him and have Sam's pack and food to carry him to civilization. He knew he could carry the green bag and his trail gear at the same time, but had seen no need in doing so while he had Eddy and Sam for pack mules.

He glanced around camp to see if there was anything lying around that he could use as a weapon. The belt hatchet caught his eye—he snatched it up and trotted out of camp, strapping it on as he went.

LIZ

Back at the Seward airport, if that flattened piece of ground and its bordering mud flats could be called such, a thoroughly pissed off FBI agent was involved in a discussion with another.

"Look, dammit, I was sent here all the way from Virginia because I know the country and I know the people. I came to help investigate—that's why they call us the Federal Bureau of Investigation, you know—not to sit on my butt in the Anchorage office and write up a report after you break the case. If you break it."

The look she received after this brazen breach of professional protocol would have taken the bark off a pine tree, but she ignored it.

"I have reason to believe a good friend of mine is on the Resurrection Trail, and is overdue. He's bit rash at times, and he could be involved with your bank robbers if they really went that way."

"Agent Nichole, we buttoned up the highway system and thoroughly checked boat and air departures. If they left Seward, it had to be by the back country, and the Resurrection Trail is the only one that gets them to civilization. If they tried to go out any other way, somebody'll find their bones later this year. We know all that, and we really don't need any extra on-scene help from you."

Elise Nichole stood there beside the helicopter, which had been borrowed from the Army for this occasion. She was armed, dressed in tactical gear, and had her flak vest hanging from her arm.

She was about to brush the other agent aside and shoulder her way on board when the local Special Agent in Charge exited the metal-clad shack that was being used as an operational center by Federal officials.

"What?" he asked, noting the contention in both faces. The male agent explained that the lady from the east was trying to force her way onto HIS aircraft.

"You have title to that Huey, huh? I'd bet the Army might disagree with you on that. Got room for Liz?"

When the agent reluctantly answered in the affirmative, the SAIC waved her aboard.

"Just don't get killed," he advised her. Turning to her former opponent,

"That lady was stationed in Alaska longer than you've been with the Bureau. She's busted some big cases and has fired a few rounds in anger. Not a good idea to get crossways with her—but you just do what you think is best."

When the chopper lifted off a few minutes later, Liz was in the door gunner's seat, binoculars in hand, looking out at the south end of the Resurrection Trail. Within a minute after takeoff, she called to the pilot to hover over a spot about a quarter-mile from the trailhead. Five minutes later, the aircraft was squatting in the road and Liz was leading the way to the truck which had been run off the road and abandoned by the robbers.

The agent who had objected to her presence was very quiet and very respectful as, at her direction, he radioed a report back to the airport command post, then placed a marker in the road for the follow-up crew.

LET'S ROLL

When Marge, Eddy, and I reached the stream camp, it was mid-afternoon. We were all pretty wrung out from the stresses of the day and looking forward to a rest and a meal. Our finding the camp empty did nothing to relieve our minds or reduce our stress.

A rough inventory of the remaining gear indicated that one person had packed up and left; common sense told us that Sam had probably decided he'd be healthier elsewhere. Apparently, he'd be wealthier too—there was no sign of the money bag. Too bad he wasn't wise also.

But there was Pete, still unaccounted for and a threat to us all. If he came back here for the money after his unlucky encounter with Marge, he would have made the same deduction that we had, and would be on Sam's trail like a bloodhound.

"Eddy, you and Marge stay here and relax a while. You have my 38 and Pete probably has nothing but his muscles. I'm going up the trail and try to keep him from killing Sam, if I can. If he shows up here, don't talk to him—shoot him."

"That's bullshit Ben. He's already ambushed you once today; if he does it again and gets your rifle, he'll work on getting us all. Nobody'll be safe.

"I'll go with you—if we space out five yards on the trail, he'll never be able to take one of us out before the other nails him."

"Hey, Eddy, you're learning. Sound like an old infantryman! But who's gonna look after Marge while we're gone?"

He was silent for a moment, thinking. He didn't finish the thought before Marge interrupted.

"Any reason I can't go along too? I've still got the 22 and I've proved I'll shoot him if I have to, maybe in a better place."

It was hard to argue with her logic. I nodded, rummaged through the scattered camping gear, and collected a few more candy bars for the trail.

"OK, grab what you need and let's roll."

THE HATCHET

Pete was moving fast, not at a run but a half trot, dropping to a walk whenever he got out of breath. The tiredness that was slowly overcoming his body seemed to dull the dozens of spots of pain that had gotten worse over the last hour. Strangely enough, the bullet wound was the least painful of the many injuries which gnawed at him.

'Guess they don't call me a "hard-ass" for nothing,' he thought to himself, then chuckled. 'Guess it's good I can find something to laugh at today. I'll find more when I catch up with Sam.'

He caught up with Sam much sooner than he thought.

Despite his newfound energy and positive attitude, it wasn't in Sam's nature to work hard when no one was pushing him. He had fallen back into his usual slow stroll, was mentally spending bundles of cash, and had no hint of Pete's presence until the blow landed on the right side of his head.

When he regained awareness, Sam was staring at the sky, a large portion of which was obscured by Pete's head and shoulders. His vision was blurred, his ears rang, and he was no longer wearing his pack.

"Where's the damn money!" The words came out garbled and slurred, but there was no mistaking what they meant.

Sam was silent, not so much in resistance, but because he was having trouble assembling his thoughts.

'Money, green bag, heavy, bank, dragged', the words bounced around in his mind until Pete kicked him hard in the ribs, then slapped his face.

"Pete, quit it," he groaned, "What did I do?"

"You stole my damn money, Shithead, where is it?" This came out somewhat clearer as Pete learned to talk around the pain.

"I. . . where was I going? Why are we stopping here?"

"Get it together, Sam. You stashed the bank money and took off toward Cooper Landing. You see this?"

He produced the little camp hatchet he had been carrying in its belt sheath.

"If you don't start remembering where the money is, I'm gonna start cutting things off until you do."

Things began to clear in Sam's mind, partly from stark fear, partly in recovery from the vicious blow Pete had delivered to the side of his head. He cast aside any hopes of keeping the money for himself—his concern now was how he might stay alive even if he did tell Pete what he wanted to know. The only reason Pete would need him now was as a hostage, and maybe to carry the money bag.

He felt his left hand being held, then pulled out away from his body. Pete was kneeling beside him, holding the hatchet ready.

"Hey, don't! Let me think a minute. That punch messed up my head."

"You don't get on with telling me what I want to know, we're gonna have two Sams half the size with one leg apiece!" This last was perfectly understandable, if not by the words, by the clear intent.

"OK, OK, just listen up a minute while I get my head straight!"

Sam thought a few more moments, and began.

"When you left camp coming this way you saw a small knobby hill on the right not too far off the trail. It was split by a real narrow cut with a little stream running out. The top was real flat."

Pete nodded. Sam continued.

"Go up in the little gorge. High on the right is some kinda animal hole in the bank. I pushed it up into that hole and shoved some dirt and rocks over it."

Pete released Sam's hand and stood. Sam tried to rise, but was pushed back by Pete's boot. Pete stood staring at Sam, shifting the hatchet from hand to hand.

Sam realized at that second that he should have given only very vague directions so that Pete would have made him actually show the way

"Damn thief!" Pete growled, swinging the hatchet at Sam's unprotected throat.

CHOPPER

Just as Eddy, Marge, and I were about to leave camp on our pursuit of Sam and Pete, I heard the old familiar whop-whop-whop of a Huey helicopter in the distance. We moved into the open on the river bank and waited to determine its course. I knew it might not be in any way connected to the law enforcement or to the robbery, but if it was, and we could flag it down, it would be a Godsend to us.

The chopper was moving slowly on a course offset from the river, swinging closer at intervals as though checking spots of interest. It had to be searching, perhaps for the robbers, perhaps for missing hikers, but it didn't really matter as long as they found us.

We made ourselves comfortable, nibbled on what food we had scrounged from the deserted camp, and awaited rescue.

It was well over an hour before the chopper worked its way to us. It was going slowly enough to give anyone on the ground who wanted to be found ample time to make their way to a clearing and signal. Anyone who didn't want to be found had plenty of forest to hide in, so the searchers weren't solely concerned with the bank robbers. The wanted any hikers picked up, probably to protect them from the gang.

When the Huey finally reached us, we were in plain view and had our thumbs extended like hitch-hikers. That's when it dawned on me that there was no good place to set the ship down, just brush, swamp, and much-too-small clearings on the shore of the river. They eased in low, and hovered in plain view. I could see the cabin was crowded and was able to recognize Russfield, Cinthia, and Whitmore waving at us through the wide gunner's door. I knew they were trying to tell us that there was no room—they'd have to make a return trip to pick us up.

On leaving, they moved slowly over us, the downwash ripping at our clothing and equipment, dropped us a flagged cannister, and slid away down-river.

I retrieved the message can and read the note inside:

> *We picked up your friends. Will be back for you after off-loading them and fueling up. Fugitives still at large. Be aware! See you in an hour or two.*
> *BEN: CAN'T YOU STAY OUT OF TROUBLE?*
> *You seem OK; I'll come back with enough gear to walk out with you if alright.*
>
> Agent Elise Nichole
> Federal Bureau of Investigation

My mouth fell open, and I must have worn a smile that split my face in two. Eddy and Marge gazed at me in wonder, waiting in silence for an explanation. When I gave it, they were astounded.

"Let's not get too cheerful," I warned, "there's still a bad guy around. I hope he hasn't run into Sam, but if he has, Sam's probably dead by now and Pete's trying to figure how to get himself and the bank money back to civilization."

CRY WOLF!

Pete was nearly to the little hill that Sam had described when he heard the helicopter. He holed up in a thicket while it did its dance over their camp, then spun away down river. He assumed that chopper would be back, perhaps after fueling, to continue its search or to pick up hikers. He needed to find the money and get the hell out of here, or to hide until the chopper either quit the search or searched someplace else.

Lying there in the bush, Pete wished he hadn't used the hatchet on Sam. For one thing, Sam could have carried the money bag and saved Pete some work. And why had he whacked Sam in the throat? The hatchet had sliced to the spine, ripping through plumbing and arteries. The arteries had immediately began pumping a miniature fountain of blood, nastily soaking Pete's skin, and clothing before he could stand and move away.

'Oh, well,' he thought, 'better his blood than mine. I can probably wash most of it out in the river before I get to Cooper Landing. But in the meantime, it does attract bugs!'

The Huey now being well out of sight and hearing, he stood and continued toward the cleft in the flat hill that Sam had described. Climbing up into the cleft, following the small brook, was easy enough. 'Had to be,' he thought, 'or Sam couldn't have done it.' The Huey had been gone over 30 minutes now—he'd better get a move on if he wanted to get back under the trees before it made another pass.

He spotted a disturbance in the dirt high on the right side of the cut which seemed likely, climbed up, brushed loose rubble out of the way, and breathed a sigh of relief. He rolled the bag out to where he could examine it, checked the exterior, and unzipped it for a look at all the bundles of green nestling inside. He stirred the money with his hands, reveling in the feel of wealth.

His joy was interrupted by a tickling on his ear and he slapped at the presumed insects, cursing the sticky blood that seemed to entice them. Feeling another on his neck, he swung a mighty slap. Instead of neck or insect, his blow contacted a furry creature which gave a sharp puppy squeal as it rolled down the bank toward the stream. A second pup, sniffing his bloody trousers, received a kick which sent it ki-yi'ing down the bank. The third had been attempting to lick blood from his clothing when Pete grasped it by the neck and one leg and flailed it against the rocky ground. The wolf pup squalled pitifully until a large gray form launched itself from above, 90 pounds of fangs and fury striking Pete squarely in the chest. Knocked backward, Pete used his all his strength to heave the female wolf off of him, the two of them rolling and sliding to the bottom of the draw. Before Pete could rise, she was on him again, fastening her fangs into his throat and doing the same work that his hatchet had done on Sam hours before.

Pete struggled; his great strength enabled him to pitch the wolf bitch off again, but she scrambled back and tore into the thing that had threatened her pups. She was biting and ripping at will and Pete grew weaker by the second, his spurting blood mixing with that of Sam Duncan. Pete died unwillingly, but die he did, less than two minutes after he had struck the first wolf pup. The mother wolf gave his body a few extra shakes, sending it rolling further down into the stream bed. She took no interest in the corpse, no longer a threat, called and nuzzled her pups, and led them away to their den further up the defile.

LET'S WALK

When the helicopter returned an hour and a half after dropping us the note, it hovered over the previous spot while Liz sat in the gunner's door signaling to us. She pointed down, signaled "no", then pointed upstream and spoke to the pilot over the intercom. The Huey spun slightly to its right and lined up on a peculiar flat- topped hill that sat by itself off the east side of the trail. Liz signaled a positive, and the chopper moved over to the hill, approached it from the east, and settled to earth. It appeared to be a half-hour's walk or so from our camp, so we gathered all the gear except mine and carried it up the trail. We turned off and found an old game trail that gave good walking and passed closest to the hill at the southeast side, near the chopper's resting place.

I halted our party before we got within hearing distance of the crew.

"Marge, do you want Eddy to go to jail?"

She looked at me in surprise, then in shock.

"I never thought about that," she replied. After thinking a few seconds, "Hell, no!"

"Eddy, do you want to go to jail?"

Eddy shook his head adamantly.

"Wait here."

I walked up to the Huey alone. Liz was standing by the left skid, no one near her. She was dressed for the trail, rather than for duty. I approached as stiffly and as official-looking as I could manage.

"Agent Nichole, may I talk to you over here for a moment?"

Liz, who had been about to jump into my arms, picked up on the game and went into character.

"Certainly, sir." She followed me back to my party and its gear.

I formally introduced her to Marge, explaining that Marge was one of the hikers that the robbers had taken prisoner on the trail.

"One of the robbers," I said, "was an unwilling member of the gang. When the leader had us lined up for the kill, me included, this third robber opened fire on him. Then, after I was freed, he helped me try and run down the leader and capture or kill him."

She looked at me with a question in her eyes.

"I don't want him to go to jail. This lady was one of the captives, one that the leader had pretty ugly plans for. She doesn't want him to go to jail either."

"Why are you asking me?" Liz questioned, although I was sure she knew the answer.

"You know a lot more about this federal law stuff than I do. If you figure he can cooperate, give testimony, and get off suspended, I'll run him down and turn him over to you. If you figure he'll have to do time, I won't."

She glanced at Eddy, who remained silent.

"This gentleman," I said, "has volunteered to escort this lady to Seward on foot if she wishes to finish her recreational wilderness trek. Whether or not they decide to continue their acquaintance afterward, I have no idea. Just as I'm quite willing to accompany you if you wish to continue hunting for the three bank robbers along the trail back to Seward."

Liz mentally chewed my little speech for a while, then responded.

"I can't say for sure what the system might decide in a matter of this nature. I'd have to do a little research back in Seward. If you can give me a few days after I return, I could probably advise you whether you should hunt him down or not."

"Fair enough; Liz, are we walking out?"

"You have a tent and a sleeping bag?"

"Just one of each."

"That's enough; let's go."

CASH FLOW

The wolf family had panicked at the sight and sound of the helicopter, and had cowered in their den after it landed. Pete's body lay unseen, 20 feet down in the bottom of the cleft on the west end of the flat-topped hill. The green money bag lay open, part of its contents strewn about the arena where the struggle had taken place.

The Huey's Army flight crew had no passengers for the return trip, both couples having elected to walk back to Seward. Strange goings on, the crew thought, but who could tell about civilians? Sometimes they showed no logic at all.

The Warrant Officer who piloted the ship figured his guys could use a break, called for lunch and fresh air. The three soldiers enjoyed an uncommon leisurely lunch hour in the sun, surrounded by some of Alaska's most spectacular scenery. By the time they were ready to take off again and resume military routine, the civilians had been gone for well over an hour. The Skipper called his men aboard and spun up the machinery.

Hearing the rotor wind up, the wolves again cowered in their den, the pups shivering in fear as the whop-whop noise got louder. Finally, the Huey lifted into the air, tilted forward, and blasted away from earth.

During takeoff, the downwash from the blades of a Huey military helicopter can impart velocities as high as 3000 feet per second to dust, dirt, and other lightweight objects and particles. When the Skipper smacked the throttle open, the downwash poured into the narrow cleft in the west end of the hill and transformed it into a natural wind tunnel. The air blast lifted and spun the green bag, spewing out its contents and bursting new bills out of the fissure like a geyser spews steam.

The crew was unconscious of their unwitting contribution to the nation's cash-flow, their attention being forward and to the sides. When the aircraft swung south and steadied on course to Seward, it left a tornado of ready cash swirling in the air over a square mile of wilderness.

Pete, if he noticed, didn't say a thing.

HONEYMOON

Liz had brought along a light pack for herself. I was to discover that it contained numerous trail goodies which were much more edible that what remained of my own food stock. A bottle of Tanqueray gin was included as well as a small thermos of ice cubes and a few take-apart plastic martini glasses.

"Nothing like roughing it in the forest primeval," I commented.

"If you think we're being too civilized," Liz responded, "I could pour it into the river and make the fish happy?"

"Or, you could just pour it into me and make me happy."

We had walked about an hour after the chopper dipped in and saluted us on its way home. I was anxious for an early camp and an early renewal of our old intimacy, but wanted a safe camp. We were sure Pete and Sam had gone north toward Cooper Landing, and in any case, were no longer armed, but I wasn't about to risk Liz to some possible desperate action on their part.

Marge and Eddy had left ahead of us. I assumed they planned to overnight at the site of my tree hugging adventure, but wasn't sure. I felt that I had watched a connection being made during the time they were together, and I had deliberately arranged things so they would have a chance to improve on it if they chose. I didn't mention this to Liz—I didn't want to hear her laughing at the idea of me matchmaking.

I stopped at the faint trail leading up to Pete's chosen killing ground, the pretty little bowl-with-a-view on the side of the mountain.

"Let's go up here. It's a pretty place to camp with a small stream, and I'll explain to you why I don't want a certain person to go to jail."

When we reached the bowl and divested ourselves of our gear, I gave serious attention to demonstrating how much I had missed her since our last meeting. Her own enthusiasm was reassuring—when your lover is five thousand miles away and working in an office crowded with eligible civilized lawyer-types, you tend to feel a bit insecure.

I sat us down at the edge of the bowl, in the place Pete had put us when he was ready for murder. I then told her the story in every detail, re-enacting where appropriate, showed her the gray mark where Pete's shotgun slug had ricocheted off the rock, and I walked her down to where the third robber (still un-named to her) had appeared and put a stop to Pete's plan.

We walked down to where Pete had fired and blown up the sawed-off shotgun. To my surprise, it still lay where he had dropped it. I picked it up and took it back to the bowl for a closer look. I remarked at the crude work which had been done on such a finely crafted shotgun. The right barrel and lock assembly were still intact—most of the left side was probably still buried in parts of the owner's body—and hurting like hell, I hoped.

When I saw the words, "James Purdey and Sons" on the right lock plate, I groaned out loud.

"What's the problem?" Liz asked.

"You probably won't get it," I said, "but this maker was an artist. His work is worth tens of thousands of dollars to serious collectors of fine antique arms. That ass chopped it up to rob a bank; if he had known to sell it, he wouldn't have needed to rob a bank.

"I see. It's like someone using a Rembrandt painting to patch a hole in the roof when he could have sold it and bought a new house."

"You've got it! I'm glad Master Purdey can't see this."

"Maybe he did, and that's why it happened."

It was too early for philosophy, so I didn't follow up on that thought. We pitched camp and had a few vermouth-less martinis and a tasty meal, followed by a single-tent, single sleeping bag honeymoon.

SUBSISTENCE

The disruption of the lives of the wolf family by humankind had been forgotten, and the pups explored their surroundings with more and growing energy. As the body in the lower part of the rocky cleft ripened, it began to draw the interest of those many creatures, large and small, which subsist on the recently living. The insects came, feasting on that part of the corpse which interested them and left eggs, shortly to become larvae, which would blindly but enthusiastically nibble even more flesh from the bones.

A wolverine wandered in, took a sample, then a meal, then settled in and defended his cache from any creature large enough to fight. When he finally left, the pups returned, tussling, and playing with the delightfully smelly parts that remained. A porcupine dropped by, licked whatever tasted salty, and ate Pete's boots and belt. A curious wolf pup learned about quills, and the indignant porky grunted his way back to open air.

A magpie scented food and fluttered down, alighting on a leg bone. Its raucous chatter drew others, which, in turn, attracted a noisy squadron of ravens. The blood-soaked clothing had long been consumed or ripped away, and the body was open to all comers.

The mother wolf disinterestedly observed all the goings on, moving to shoo her pups away only while the wolverine was in residence. Had she been very hungry, she might have joined the freeloaders who feasted on the fruits of her anger, but she preferred her meat fresher, and she disliked the man-smell.

LAWYERING

Marge, Eddy, and I sat with Liz in a bar booth in mid-town Seward. Liz had collected us to hear the results of her research on the possibility of the "third robber" testifying and getting off with no jail time. The bar was noisy with people who had congregated to celebrate or mourn the performance of their favorite Marathon Race runners. A gentleman named Bill Spencer seemed to have won the honors this year, and many glasses were tipped and toasts made to that gentleman. We attracted no attention at all.

"Ben," Liz began, "this is a ticklish situation. The powers that be, and that includes local and state authorities, not just the FBI, would agree to immunity from prosecution if the testimony results in arrest of the robbers and the return of the money."

"Hell, Liz—that isn't gonna work and you know it. He can identify them and tell you the details of the plan, but he can't run off into the hills and bring them in. And if he doesn't know where they are, how would he know where the money is? From what I saw, one ran off toward Cooper with the money bag and the other took off to catch him and get the money back. Which probably means that at least one is now dead, and I'd bet it's Sam"

"Good question. And I don't have an answer."

"Doesn't saving the lives of four people at the risk of one's own rate extra credit? If what he did hadn't been connected to the bank robbery, they'd give him a medal for it. Are they saying that the bank's money is worth more than four human lives? If our man thought so, I and at least three others would be rotting on that mountainside. And Marge here would have been violated and killed. Make that five lives!"

"Damn, Ben—you ought to go and make that argument to the brass. You're coming across like a good lawyer, but one without a legal leg to stand on."

"Liz, if they want to jail him for being a hero, I'm gonna let him stay on the run. He's a better citizen than most of the people who are so damn interested in just getting their money back. And I'm gonna talk to the press about it if nobody else will listen."

"Ben," she ordered," get up off your butt and come with me. Now!"

Surprised at the peremptory tone of her voice, I stood. She took my arm, threw a bill on the table, and steered me out of the bar.

"You persuaded me," she said, "but I don't count. You're going to come and persuade the people that I answer to."

I don't know exactly how she engineered it, but the next morning I stood in front of the Mayor, the bank president, the local Police Chief, the SAIC of the Anchorage FBI office, the senator representing the Seward district, a lady from the State Adjutant General's office, and a newspaper reporter from Anchorage.

Liz steered me through the same basic arguments I had used with her at the bar yesterday, and having me repeat and emphasize the most telling points.

The audience asked a few questions on some of the less-clear points, and one tried to imply that I might have had some connection with the robbery. Another hinted that I might be charged with obstructing justice if I didn't give the "third man" up. The words, "Fuck you!" were on the tip of my tongue, but I managed to stay silent. If he could have read my thoughts, he'd have made it a point never to cross my path.

Liz stepped to the front.

"Mister Hunnicutt, have you talked to the press about this affair?"

"No, Ma'am."

"Do you intend to?"

"Not unless I feel that an injustice has been done here."

She sat down.

There were no more questions; we were dismissed.

RELOCATION

A pair of hikers heading north on the Resurrection Trail came upon the body of Sam Duncan. They rolled him off the trail and marked the spot with a toilet paper flag visible from the air. Upon reaching the Russian River trail head some days later, they dutifully notified an Alaska Trooper who was busy looking for unlicensed fishermen, over-bag-limit poachers, and snaggers. Any break from having to deal with whining, excuse-making, so-called sportsmen was welcome. The brown-shirted Trooper, hoping the incident wasn't a false alarm, alerted his boss by radio—requesting at the same time that he be allowed to resume his blue-shirt law-enforcement rotation and accompany the investigators.

Ecstatic when his request was approved, he rushed off to change uniforms and join the chopper crew that would be dispatched to the scene.

When the helicopter crew spotted the toilet paper flag, they marked it on a map in case they couldn't find a spot to land. After circling the area, it was obvious to them that the only safe landing zone was on a flat-topped rocky hill about an hour from the body. The winds being from the west, the chopper approached the hill from the east, flared, and settled on the hilltop.

The Troopers had noted a game trail on the south side of the hill which seemed to lead to the main trail. Carrying a stretcher, body bag, and the usual crime scene equipment, they set off on their search.

The wolf family again cowered in its den; the noise and wind signaled threats foreign to their experience, enemies that the female wolf was not ready to challenge. Some hours later, the Troopers returned with their grisly burden, their cameras filled with images of a bloody corpse after a coyote family had finished with it.

When the helicopter lifted off westward, the redistribution of wealth repeated itself. Bills still in bundles had not blown far on the first occasion—now the thin bands which had restrained them had been exposed to the weather. The downwash from the rotors popped the bands; newly freed bills fluttered away into the river, streams, and bogs, decorated the trees, and spun away to settle in small hidden valleys. Loose bills that had been well distributed by the first Huey lift-off got a second wind, flying and fluttering another quarter-mile, and waiting for the next local windstorm to send them further.

Again, the chopper crew's attention was to the front and sides—they had no idea of the rich heritage they had left behind.

The mother wolf led her mate and her pups across the valley in search of a new denning area. She had had enough of humans and the complications they gave to a simple thing like living.

IMMUNITY

After we left the jury of my non-peers, Liz drove me by the Brandt home to collect my truck, and to visit with young Jody. Gary was away doing his shift on the Alaska Railroad, so Liz chatted with Nina while I passed the time away being pummeled by Jody, and trying to answer the endless unanswerable questions that a young mind dreams up.

There had been little change in the Brandt family or their lives, except that their young son seemed a foot taller and 20 pounds heavier than when I last saw him. His father was a giant, well over six feet tall with flowing blonde hair and the appearance of a Viking raider—I expected young Jody to be a match.

Nina's sister, Dora, had been the fiancé of my friend and first Operation Washtub recruit, Joe Doane. Dora had been murdered along with Joe back in 1956, and I had met the Brandts while trying to track down Joe's killer. We had been friends ever since.

When we left the Brandts, I asked Liz to meet me in yesterday's bar; we'd walk up to a diner and have lunch. She had to check in with her office first, but agreed to lunch, not a diner, but in a sit-down restaurant. A half-hour later, I walked up toward the bar, mentally trying to devise a means of tricking her into paying the lunch tab.

I was sitting at the bar, my beer only down by two inches when she came bustling in, Eddy and Marge in tow.

"Ben," she said as we slid into the same booth we had vacated yesterday, "You need to go to law school. I just got a message saying that the panel was convinced—they'll go along with the immunity agreement."

She turned to Eddy with her hand out. "Congratulations!"

"What do you mean congratulations? Why are you so sure I'm the third robber?"

"Aw, come on, Eddy—that's why they appointed me an investigator. I investigate stuff. And I could read it in Marge's face without half trying."

Marge leaned over and gave Eddy a non-platonic kiss on the mouth; he tried not to return it, but gave up and pulled her to him. Liz gave me a grin, followed by a twin to Marge' kiss.

"Say," Marge asked, "what would you have done if Eddy had been turned down?"

"Why, Marge, I wouldn't have had the slightest idea that it was Eddy," said Liz. "I'd have sent Ben out to chase down whoever it was— like he said he'd do." She looked at me.

"And I'd have done it too," I said, "Probably have started on the trail some time during the next month or two, after Liz went back to Virginia."

Noting the puzzled looks from the couple, Liz went on to explain our 5000-mile romantic relationship, and how it had begun. By the time she had finished the somewhat involved story, my beer was down another six inches and I was hungry.

"Let's eat," I said. "But first—Liz, I'll bet you lunch for everybody that I can guess which of my arguments convinced your panel to give Eddy a break." She thought the challenge over for a few seconds, then nodded.

"You're on!"

"It was my statement that I might contact the press if I thought justice was not being served."

She swung around with eyes like the turret guns of a light cruiser.

"You cheating Es Oh Bee! Who told you?"

"I'm a student of human nature, my dear. I knew some in that room were for giving the third man a break, some hard against. But right or wrong had nothing to do with it. Except for that reporter, everybody in that room was some sort of a politician. And not a one was willing to jail a hero and face public opinion."

"Now let's go; I'm getting hungry, and I'm sure Eddy and Marge are too."

SEWARD

Marge, as the rescued victim of a criminal gang, was treated with kindness and sympathy by the citizens of Seward. She was immediately offered employment by a number of businesses who could profit by having a buxom, attractive blonde in a receptionist's office or across a counter.

Eddy was known to have had some part in the hunt for the bank robbers, but law enforcement officials, for once, stayed close-mouthed about the details. Eddy was offered a job as a parts runner for a local auto parts business. The job not only required getting to know many local businesses, but making weekly runs to other towns on the Kenai and to suppliers in Anchorage. His face soon became well known in automotive and industrial circles throughout south-central Alaska.

Eddy Hoyt seemed taller and more self-confident as he and Marge were seen together around Seward; people readily recognizing and speaking to the gentleman that once would have been a mere face in a crowd. There was once a rumor that Eddy had been arrested in Anchorage for being drunk and disorderly, but it didn't seem to sully his reputation for honesty and trustworthiness. To a large segment of the Seward population, being drunk and disorderly in Anchorage indicated a streak of independence and gumption.

SEWARD, SIX YEARS LATER

Pete Peterson's bones lay scattered in the narrow defile until the spring following his demise. That spring, the spring of 1976, followed a winter of extreme snow in the mountains which formed the Resurrection River valley. The abrupt melting of that snow was due to unusually warm spring winds, and the result was a tremendous runoff into the local streams and rivers.

The water that sluiced down the mountainside turned the little defile where he lay into a torrent that swept the stream bed clean, all the way down to bedrock. Pete's bones, now disconnected and scattered, tumbled down the slope to the valley bottom below, where they lingered throughout a hot, dry summer, bleaching in the sun.

Another winter with less snow and more rain fed the swollen streams and pushed Pete's bones into the rushing Resurrection River. They were tumbled along the river bed, the sandy bottom scouring and the silty waters polishing. Each bone its own relic now, some were buried on sand bars, some hung on sunken stumps and boulders, some continued to roll and bounce downstream toward the salty sea beyond.

Ed and Marge Hoyt, along with their five-year old son, Benny, were enjoying a picnic on a gravel bar near the Resurrection River trailhead. The beautiful sunny weather, a sudden change from the gray overcast of the previous week, had prompted Ed to take a day off from his duties as Assistant Manager of a local auto parts store. Marge was lying back on a blanket enjoying the warmth of the afternoon sun. Ed watched her, something like adoration in his eyes.

He reached over, pulled up her maternity top, kissed the smooth tightness of her belly—and abruptly sat up.

"The little devil kicked me," he exclaimed, then bent down and put his face against her.

"Whoops, he did it again."

"You're sure it was a he? Girls can kick too," she said.

"Felt masculine to me. Did you come up with any names yet?"

"Well, I think it's a girl. I was thinking maybe "Elise", after Liz Nichole. She did a lot for us."

"Elise Hoyt. Liz Hoyt," He savored the sounds. "Not a bad ring to it. You're sure you don't want "Marjorie"?"

"I hear that enough. Let's not inflict it on our daughter—if there is one. But if it's another boy?"

"Well, you once suggested Edward Hoyt Junior. I'll buy Eddy Hoyt or Ed Hoyt, as long as we don't call him "Junior"! You don't think it might be twins . . .?"

"Daddy, Daddy, look what I found!"

Benny was running toward them from the edge of the water clutching a shiny bowl-like object in his arms. When he arrived, he dropped the object on the blanket beside them. Marge recoiled in horror; Ed was startled, but picked up the object with interest.

"A human skull. Where'n hell could this have come from?"

"Language, Eddy," Marge admonished, propriety taking precedence over horror for the moment.

"Whose do you think it was?" asked Benny, not at all disturbed by the grisly nature of his prize.

The jawless skull merely stared at them in silence.

"I don't know. Maybe some hunter or trapper who froze to death, or was caught in a snow slide."

"Maybe an Indian, or somebody that was killed by a bear, or . . .?" Benny ran out of victims about which to speculate.

"I dunno. Guess we'll have to take it in to the police and let them check it out."

"Aw, Daddy—they won't know. Can I keep it? Might be somebody that was killed by a wolf who ate everything but his head."

Ed smiled.

"No, son, wolves won't harm humans. Everybody knows that."

Pete, if he heard, said not a word.

THE END

Author's Notes

The story you just read is very loosely based on the actual robbery of the Seward branch of the 1st National Bank at 2:40 PM on August 4th, 1971. Three robbers hit the bank, scooping up an amount which has yet to be confirmed by the bank, but which weighed 40 pounds or more when packed in a green rubberized duffle bag. A sawed-off shotgun was used, a violation of federal law, and 25 FBI agents descended on the scene to help the five-man police force and the Alaska State Troopers in their search.

Since there was (and is) only one road out of Seward, the gang expected to escape cross country. They were unsuccessful, were caught, and were convicted and sentenced to six years each. Their leader was out on probation in four years and kept his nose clean, as far as we know, for 20 more. He was then convicted of a double murder near Talkeetna and was sentenced to well over a hundred years in prison, which he is still serving at a prison near Seward.

The loot was all recovered, so it will do no good for readers to hike the Resurrection Trail in the hope of plucking money off of trees. If they go only for the beauty of the land, however, they will be richly rewarded.

Don Neal
6 September 2020